A small aircraft battling a sudden storm above the terrible Alaskan wilderness... ...

.....A rainsquall sailed into their path just as they were poised to shoot between the two peaks. Colburn hesitated and then decided to go on. If visibility worsened he would have a few minutes to turn back. Farther on, though, the Gap narrowed and there would be no room to complete a turn. The plane poked hesitantly into the squall, rain rattling on the wings and fuselage like gravel. The ground rushed beneath in a blur of rock and ice. Rain smothered the windshield, the frantic wipers scraping it away in curling streamers that exploded into mist past the side windows. Colburn cursed his decision to go on. No margin of safety remained – they were taking an appalling risk. A part of him seemed to detach and hover over himself, scolding, "This is how it happens."

Sea-Change
And Other Stories

By Dave Parmenter

CONTENTS

To Mark,

Who knows why

Or should.....

PREFACE

When I came of age as a young surfer in the 1970s I devoured every surf magazine I could get my hands on. They were few and far between back then, and the arrival of a new issue of *Surfer Magazine* every two months was something like a religious holiday in the still underground surf culture.

As a voracious bookworm feasting on Ray Bradbury and Jules Verne and Ian Fleming, I was astonished at the high level of writing in the surf periodicals back then. Aside from the fact that the bulk of the writing back then was actual journalism (however gonzo), they printed quite a bit of short fiction. But by the time I began contributing articles to the surf magazines in 1981 that golden age of surf writing had come to a close and over the ensuing years it seemed more and more that being a 'surf writer' meant little more than being a poorly paid copywriter for the surf industrial complex whose companies' advertisements had become the *raison d'etre* for the once radical, counterculture American glossies.

As a budding writer it was hard to miss out on that era of provocative fiction and Imagineering - and as I climbed the mastheads at various magazines through the years I vowed to sneak in elements of short fiction or whenever possible even bits and pieces of legitimate literature.

Fortunately circa 1991 a new editor at *Surfer*, Steve Hawk, set out to cultivate if not *bona fide* literature at least proper journalism in the Bible of the Sport. Hawk brought to bear his newspaper background and created a very writer-friendly environment and encouraged his editorial staff to swing for the fences. In this environment I was encouraged to expand the boundaries of standard fill-in-the-blanks surf mag boilerplate, and turn in fresh copy that challenged the readership a bit.

Years later, encouraged by my rapport with Hawk as my editor, I was lucky to work with a number of other tremendously farsighted and pro-literature editors. Steve Pezman, Scott Hulet, Evan Slater, and especially my good friend Chris Mauro handed me *carte blanche* and stepped back to let me have at it. The bulk of the stories collected here appeared in Pezman's and Hulet's peerless *The Surfers' Journal* (though they rejected *Sanctuary* - it appears here for the first time). *Bluebirds At Midnight* originally ran in *Surfer*, though in a slightly different form since it was solely designed to be a bio piece about Duke Kahanamoku. I liked the Ray Bradbury-esque hook of the story and rewrote it a few years after it appeared in *Surfer*.

The titular story of this collection, *Sea-Change*, came about as the result of a photograph my friend Dr. Mark Renneker sent me. It depicted him in a lonely camp on the shores of southeastern Alaska, a wilderness he thrives in above all other places. Looking at the picture I sensed a sort of melancholy in his aspect, and suddenly had an insight as to why he went to such raw cold places as Alaska, Norway, Iceland, and even the Antarctic. Immediately there came an urge to write a story about it, and right off the bat I felt that I wanted the story to crawl on the page gently and decently like one of Nevil Shute's understated novels.

The story ended up going through numerous drafts and many revisions and ended up in length qualifying as more of a novella than a short story. I rewrote the first draft from stem to stern after discovering it was apparent that I had written a crackling adventure story about flying in Alaska - but by doing so I was hiding from my original theme. It was painful to face that theme. Renneker is a brilliant and compassionate oncologist who deals each day with stricken patients like the fictional Ellen Kawena in the story. Along with an equally brilliant and compassionate friend of us both, Dr. Keith Block, Renneker walked at the side of my late wife, Rell Sunn, as she struggled with the same plight as Ellen in *Sea-Change*.

I once asked Renneker how he was able to cope, each and every day, with such heartrending suffering and live-and-death decisions. Knowing that I was an aviation enthusiast, he replied quite simply that it was like piloting an airplane by instruments alone. You used your training and experience and the gauges in front of you to direct your decisions and keep the plane level - to look out the window into zero visibility was to invite spatial disorientation and disaster. With this analogy I knew he was telling me it was dangerous to get emotionally involved to the point where the logic and protocols learned in one's training might be endangered. Physicians have to fly IFR. That idea formed the core of the story with which I grappled.

Since the first thing an editor of a surfing magazine says upon receiving engaging short fiction is, "Liked the story - but how are we going to illustrate it?" it goes without saying that I am grateful that any of these stories were ever published. Scott Hulet at *The Surfers' Journal* found a way around that problem, especially with *Sea-Change*, and granted these stories a literary home.

Hopefully we will again witness, in some future renunciation of commercially corrupted surf writing, a return to experimentation and diversity in the surfing media, much like what has happened with independent filmmaking in the wake of the digital revolution.

Dave Parmenter
Kapaa, Hawaii
March 2013

Sea-Change

I don't know if you have ever been in a small airplane that is in trouble. I don't mean an airliner. The great passenger jets may wobble a bit here and there, tinkling the ice cubes in one's drink, but they soar well above the weather. The small plane is different. Lower down, beneath the sea of clouds, lay rain and fog and ice. Ice is especially dangerous to the pilot. One can fly blind through rain and fog on instruments but when ice spreads over the wings or jams the rudder it is all over. I learned to fly long before I became an oncologist and I have always thought of ice as similar to cancer in the way that the tiniest patch can, like a single malignant cell in a body, spread over the plane and bring it down.

I remember a younger colleague of mine, Dr. Ralph Weatherford, who became stuck in one of these traps waiting in the sky where the pilot suddenly finds, like all too many cancer patients, that he cannot go on, turn around, or safely land.

Weatherford was heading home, the solitary passenger in a little single-engine Cessna, after a surfing trip to a deserted beach in Alaska, when the weather began to clamp down. It was September and he had never been up there so late in the year. The first storm of the season was gathering force to the west, weeks early. Already the sky was blackening.

The pilot, Frank Colburn, glanced anxiously at the gauges.

"I don't know, Doc," he said. "It's getting awful soupy out there."

Things were falling apart and he knew that in a few minutes he would have to drop even lower to stay beneath the cloud ceiling. Like most of the other Alaskan bush pilots, he held an instrument flight rating but couldn't lawfully fly passengers in instrument conditions. Besides, no one in their right mind flew IFR over country like that if they could help it.

"Thought we could make it back scud running," he said. "Guess we'll have to go down to 800 feet and hope this gunk doesn't keep squeezing us down to the deck."

It was the last flight for him after a long summer of hauling hunters, anglers, and photographers into the wilderness. His off-season would begin as soon as the tires touched the runway. Now, if they lost visibility, they would have no choice but to set down on the beach somewhere.

Weatherford sat next to the pilot, in the right-hand seat, every muscle tensed as the plane bucked and plunged into the gusting headwind 1000 feet above the shoreline. They were a long way from safety and ahead he could see the leading edge of the cold front was alarmingly closer. It was going to be a near thing.

Weatherford gently shifted his cramped legs, carefully avoiding the extra set of rudder pedals on the floor. Shifting the nose of his beat-up red surfboard to the other side of his seat, he squirmed into a new position. He was too tall to be comfortable in the tiny cockpit, and already sensed the first twinges of a muscle spasm in his lower back.

A curtain of rain hung before them and in an instant they pierced it, the fat drops rattling like hail on the aircraft. Weatherford sneaked a glance at the pilot, hoping to find assurance in a normal expression. The pilot held the yoke with one hand, still with the easy, calm grip of one doodling with a pencil – yet his mouth was a tight, clamped line. Frank Colburn was a careful and methodical bush pilot with twenty years of experience in northern skies. One tends to want such a man in Alaska – it is the green pilot or overconfident veteran that gets one killed up there.

"Well," sighed the pilot, "here goes another 200 feet from our account."

They descended to 800 feet, the Cessna shuddering and rocking in the chop. Warm sea air was sloshing ashore and colliding with cold air pouring down from the immense glaciers that caked the coastal mountains. Weatherford peered out the side window at the wet black sand of the shoreline scrolling by, lined for a hundred miles with the sodden remains of countless trees. The plane rolled at a slap of wind and he saw a flash of metal gray sea beneath. Yes, the whitecaps were bigger now, he was sure of it. He turned to glance out the pilot-side window. There, buried somewhere beneath the ragged clouds foaming against its peaks, was the Desolation Range, barring them from escaping inland – many of its peaks were higher than ten thousand feet, far higher than the little Cessna could hope to climb.

At 800 feet the visibility was better – but for how long, Weatherford wondered. The danger of their situation was plain even to a non-pilot. He understood how narrow the path had become. Below was the freezing storm-torn sea. In the fixed-gear Cessna it was impossible to manage a survivable water landing and, as a surfer, Weatherford knew it was pointless anyhow. In the towering waves and icy water one would last only a few miserable minutes. Then there were the mountains foaming in the scud like rabid fangs scarcely a dozen miles off their left wing. And higher up in the air above them were the upper teeth of the closing trap, the boiling columns of cloud shoveled in by the cold front.

With a prickle of fear Weatherford noticed the tide creeping in already, surging up the beach toward the tangle of logs and driftwood that formed a barricade to turn back the sea from the forest. Even equipped with its spongy oversize beach tires the Cessna would soon have no room to land if they were forced down. And the little plane was being forced lower and lower.

The way to safety was no longer a limitless skyway but a long and narrow cavern 800 feet tall and some forty feet wide.

I've been flying since I was a boy and I can tell you that this sort of scenario still scares the hell out of me. When everything goes rotten like that it's so easy to lose your head and wad it up. And if one is flying over wilderness…

I vividly recall the time, long before I had left home to study medicine, when I was flying my father's Stearman off the strip near our place in Montana and somehow got boxed in amongst the foothills under a lowering ceiling. I had gone up to see if I could spot some stray cattle, and found them so close by that I figured I would go skylarking for a while. I lost track of the time and didn't notice how low on fuel I was, and … well, if I'm going to start 'hangar flying' I may as well stick to the story I was telling, and start from the beginning.

I first met Dr. Ralph Weatherford at an oncology conference in San Francisco. I seemed to recall that I had heard something about him, as we both had practices in the City and lived on its outskirts. He came late to the conference and sat next to me, in the middle of a somewhat pedantic lecture on anti-angiogenesis given by a researcher who had never seen a real tumor. His hair was the first thing I noticed. It was very long and tied into a loose ponytail. After a few minutes I thought I heard what sounded like a leaking faucet and noticed that water was dripping from the stalk of his ponytail and plopping onto the carpet. Not being interested in the lecture, which in any event I felt to be a dead end as far as therapies go, I directed my curiosity to my seatmate and appraised him from the corner of my eye.

He wore thick wide-wale corduroy pants, a hooded sweatshirt once bright green but now faded and pale, and had his large feet stuffed into fur-lined moccasins several sizes too small. On the sweatshirt there remained the ghostly imprint of what appeared to be a surfboard brand name, the ink long since worn away and illegible. His long and solemn face was red, in a healthy way, as if keened by a cold and bracing wind. I later found out that he'd just arrived from a morning of surfing out on the coast.

I couldn't help but think he resembled something of a cross between a Berkeley professor with a PhD in poetry and a hippie surfer. He also looked, however, to be the most vital and alive person in the entire auditorium. It struck me then that I had heard talk about him, of course. In a conservative and hidebound discipline such as oncology, one cannot help but notice the whispering and clucking of tongues amongst the white–coated herd when a fellow physician breaks away and 'goes Eastern'.

Ralph Weatherford had 'gone Eastern,' it was said. In his practice he promoted the benefits of a simple, peasant diet, and employed Chinese herbal medicines and yoga. Many of my colleagues, rooted in the somewhat medieval belief that more powerful and toxic drugs would drive out the malignant demons, dismissed Weatherford as another holistic quack who had gained a toehold in oncology during the present tolerance of unconventional therapies.

When the conference broke for lunch I introduced myself and invited him to dine with me, mostly out of curiosity, but also as a challenge to myself to keep from turning into an old fuddy-duddy. I was twenty-five years Ralph Weatherford's senior and certain we had little in common. I remember that lunch well. Outraged at the 'factory food' set before us, he pushed his plate away and produced from the pouch of his sweatshirt a slab of mixed raw nuts fused by a glop of raisins and dates into a sort of pemmican. Pronouncing my meal to be nothing more than 'modules of prefab transfats and Dow additives', he waded into a tart diatribe about the role of diet in cancer and other degenerative diseases. Somehow we were able to talk shop for an hour and in the end I found myself suitably impressed – or entertained – to agree to accompany him to an upcoming integrative cancer therapy conference, to be held the following month up the coast in Bolinas.

We got to know one another pretty well after that. I found myself quite against my will growing more and more interested in his practice. Soon we were meeting often to discuss cases and treatment options. It's strange, but I guess one could say that I sought out his counsel more than he did mine. He always tried to explain surfing to me, about how important it was to his work. I spoke to him about the passion of my youth, flying, but whenever I recommended it to him, that he might try a few lessons, he stopped me cold. It was all just more regulations, he claimed, and as a physician he was sick of them already. Why get involved in a pursuit choked by more rules, a pursuit in which only a tiny part actually was about flying a plane. I figured he was child of the Sixties, a reactionary – or just terrified of airplanes. Later, I found out he spent quite a lot of time aloft, not as a pilot, of course, but as a passenger in search of remote waves.

I came to realize, strangely enough, that we had much in common. We had both seen the glory years of our favorite pastimes come and go. Weatherford insisted that surfing, as a subculture, was finished. Overcrowding and commercialism, he contended, had stripped it of its primal tang. I had no way of gauging the accuracy of his claim, having always felt surfing to be a frivolous and youthful fad, but agreed that flying too had changed. For both of us, the thrills and dangers inherent in our respective pursuits were no longer associated with a communion with natural forces – in fact, both had sunken into being mostly concerned with the avoidance of traffic.

Just as it was true I no longer flew in the system, choosing instead to fly my father's old open–cockpit Stearman – without a radio – from our place in Montana, so too did Weatherford seek out and find his own 'uncontrolled airspace' in which to enjoy the waves.

I'm not sure how long he had been going up to Alaska. Of his longer disappearances he said little. He came and went without fanfare or comment, returning always weather-beaten but bright and cheerful. Perhaps he was being protective of some secret hoard – surfers as a rule seem to be overtly xenophobic – or maybe he was sensitive to being branded an eccentric. More likely, as he was an extraordinarily caring and sensitive physician, it may have been that he harbored a secret guilt at being so healthy and mobile, so able to freely enter and leave the wild places while his patients remained behind, trapped in wildernesses from which most would never emerge.

I had known Weatherford for a few years before he mentioned his surfing trips to Alaska. At that point I was tolerant of his eccentricities – maybe even respected them. My war on cancer, as with many of my colleagues', seemed bogged down in a stalemate, yet Weatherford's patients enjoyed higher survival times than those who went to the big expensive cancer centers.

One night after dinner Weatherford unrolled his Alaskan charts and showed me the places he had been. He raved about the empty beaches and surf. I was winding down my career then, thinking about retiring in a few years, and starting to long for the open spaces. I admit I listened impatiently to his surfing tales. I was raised on a ranch cradled by the stern and godlike Rocky Mountains and it was hard for such a confirmed landlubber to envision frolicking on a surfboard as being the equal of heading out on horseback into the meadows and valleys of the high country.

To Weatherford, though, the ocean was the greatest of wildernesses. But it wasn't until he told me he flew by bush plane and was left – utterly alone – on a remote coast, that I showed any excitement. Not about the surfing, of course. I thought only of the flying. There is some very rough country up there and the small-plane pilot is still able to fly around without a lawyer in his back pocket. From then on I always listened intently to his tales. But I also worried.

That next summer was a rotten one for Weatherford. August in San Francisco ushers in the fourth month of fog and wind and icy water. The cold northwest wind scours the coast day and night, and fogbanks stream in and cling like plaque to the shore. For the hardcore enthusiast there is little surf, and Weatherford, who lived for the big winter surf, went into a sort of mourning.

"I've got to get out of here," he told me one day in August. "For a while, at least. Might be able to manage a week if no one crash dives."

"Where are you thinking of going?" I asked. It was a Sunday, and another gloomy summer morning of thick fog. We ate breakfast at a little café near the end of Judah Street and decided to walk down to the beach.

"Alaska, I think. You know something? The weather is good up there right now. There's a nice big blob of high pressure in the Gulf. Won't be surf here for another six weeks, but it's always winter up there. Anyway…" He threw up his hands, indicating the gloom pouring in from the sea. The fog was thickening into drizzle, dripping down the windshields of cars and plastering hair onto one's forehead. The row of ice plant growing along the shore glistened and gave off the cloying sweet smell of a stopped-up drain.

We sat down on a bench overlooking one of his favorite surf breaks. Weatherford was disgusted. Though the ocean was invisible, screened off by the curtain of fog, he claimed it was befouled by a red tide. He could smell it - the brown-red algae gave him sinus trouble, one of the reasons he hated the summer. After a long silence he spoke:

"You remember that patient I told you about last week?" he said. "Kellerman. Prostate with mets. Stage Four."

I recalled some of the details. We'd arranged for the man to receive proton beam therapy in Loma Linda. The patient had enjoyed some remission and almost total relief from pain.

"I got his latest scans yesterday," he went on. "He's relapsed. There's more bone involvement, and mets to his liver. I'm out of ideas, and besides, I doubt he could travel any more even if I could find something else for him. ... I've arranged it with hospice...."

He sat there, looking pale and listless. I knew it had been a bad summer for him. He had been handling a number of high-stakes cases, younger people with bleak diagnoses. Weatherford's patients were always more challenged than most. Usually they came to him after their primary physicians had given up on them, after being told there was 'nothing more that could be done.'

He had already lost two patients that summer, both young and athletic, both with families. It was an unusual spike in morbidity, though he normally worked on the end-stage tightrope.

"They always come to me too late, Walter." He shook his head. "The patient I lost in July – Hansen – I first saw when she was in hospice already. Her primary 'onc' was a moron – "

I started to protest, but he cut me short.

"Alright, alright, I can't say for certain that there was malpractice – but at the very least he was asleep at the wheel. Appalling!"

We sat there for a few minutes peering out into the gray drizzle. I had twenty-five years of practice on him; things had been much, much worse back when I had entered the field. I was grateful for the tools now at hand. Weatherford, idealistic and assured in his systemic approach, had not yet accepted that in all battles there must be some casualties.

Finally he sneezed and cleared his throat.

"When I'm out surfing, sometimes I'll come across a bee struggling in the water," he said, his voice muffled by his clogging sinuses. "In the fall, when the wind blows offshore, they get blown out to sea, and when they grow too exhausted to fly any longer they just plop down into the water. The surface tension keeps them afloat, but it also traps them."

"Suction," I nodded.

"Yes. Anyway, I'll scoop up the bee and place it on the nose of my board, out of the water, and let it rest and dry off. But its wings are wet and it's too tired. ...And if a good wave comes I forget about the bee, and it gets washed off the board."

Sometimes one would make it, he said, would dry its wings in the breeze and find the energy to buzz back to shore. Mostly they were lost, swept away, drowned. Listening to him, I began to realize he was alluding to far more than his frustrations in treating desperately ill people – he was talking about guilt, the guilt of abandoning patients with their chemo ports and bald heads and withering hopes – and flying off to rejuvenate himself in the wilderness.

"All your years in practice, Walter." He turned his eyes from the beach and looked at me. "I mean, how did you do it? How did you keep from bringing it home with you?"

I turned to face the breeze, thinking. The wind was blowing harder now and for the first time I detected the pungent briny smell of the red tide. Even the ocean got sick, I supposed. Had I, all those years ago, felt like Weatherford? No, I decided, it had been easier then. Then there were fewer options, and less understanding. Nature ran the roulette wheel, and the odds were always stacked in favor of the house. We did what we could and lived with the inevitable attrition.

I have always believed that a pilot, even one without an instrument rating, could always fly his way out of a bad situation, as long as he didn't become disoriented and panic. That was how I had always modeled my practice, the doctor as pilot, in bad weather pulling his eyes from the deceptive view outside and looking only to the instruments.

"You know, Ralph, when you fly into cloud," I said, tumbling out of my reverie, "it's best to not even look outside. You can't trust your own eyes – they'll play tricks on you. The next thing you know, you'll be flying upside down."

He was smiling ironically, a smirk that said, There he goes again with the flying stories.

"Yes, Walter, but…."

"…You'll be flying upside down," I said again, cutting him off. "Listen now. When you can't see outside all you can trust are your instruments. Airspeed. Altimeter. Heading. They're the only absolutes – the only things you can trust. That's how I've always treated cancer. I look only at the gauges – at my training – and if I do everything that is called for when it is called for, well, I'll get down safely at the other end."

"And your passenger? Your patient?"

"I know, I know. They don't always make it down with me. But that doesn't mean you have to crash with them, does it? Damn it, Ralph, the next flight leaves first thing in the morning and someone will need you in the left seat."

Weatherford didn't get to Alaska that August after all. Ironically, that 'next flight' would take him not to Anchorage but to Honolulu. The year before I had invited Weatherford to join the Tumor Board at the University of California, San Francisco. I was chairman of a small group of oncologists that sought out and reviewed unusual cases that might benefit from various clinical trials. Complementary therapies by then were edging into the mainstream, and I felt Weatherford would be a valuable addition to the Board.

Not long after our conversation at the beach a case came up for review involving a woman in Hawaii with breast cancer. How Ellen Kawena was networked to the Tumor Board at UCSF I will never know. But Weatherford knew of her through the surfing subculture. According to him, she had been an Olympic swimmer, well known to veteran surfers because of her enormous popularity in the Islands. Although only in her middle years, Miss Kawena was severely challenged by her disease. It was, admittedly, the type of situation in which Weatherford excelled. Yet I saw right away that he might become too involved. He leapt at the case, scoffing at the Board's suggestion she be placed in a high–dose chemotherapy trial at the MD Anderson Center in Texas. Time couldn't be wasted, he argued. He offered to fly to Hawaii and consult with her attending oncologist and study the latest scans and pathology reports.

There was an argument, quite vicious as I recall, about the treatment options open to Miss Kawena. Weatherford held his ground, savaging the idea of more conventional treatment, claiming that the proposed high–dose trial would flatten her. Besides, he reasoned, she had already failed two chemo regimens and likely had developed a resistance to most of the front–line cytotoxic drugs.

He flew to Honolulu two days later. I heard nothing from him while he was there. Then, ten days later he was back. I picked him up at the airport, eager to discuss the case with him, to compare notes. But he seemed dispirited and, after a few minute's desultory talk, declined my offer to have dinner, claiming he was tired and not very hungry. He disappeared from my radar screen after that.

A week later I called his office, but got only the answering machine. I left a message. His secretary got back to me the next day.

He had gone to Alaska.

Weatherford camped on the beach at the top of a low, rocky headland somewhere in southeastern Alaska. At the very edge of the beach began a thick belt of rainforest and low swampy lakes, which ended abruptly at the base of Mount Foraker, a massive shark tooth of a mountain towering out of the coastal range that holds back the ice of the Canadian interior. His tent was pitched amid a jumble of room–sized squares of rock, blocks of granite stranded by ancient glaciers long vanished into the sea. On sunny days he liked to lay on a warm rock and read, though he never got through more than a paragraph before his eyes were drawn once again to the looming presence of Mount Foraker. He had never seen the mountain. Its peak was ever tufted in cloud, gray on the stormy days and downy white on fine days. But the pile of cloud only made it seem larger, more mysterious, and he longed for the day he would finally see it. Weatherford claimed to go there for the isolation and the tapering waves that broke along the boulders beside his camp - but more than anything, I think, he hungered to have his existence shrunk by the hugeness of the North.

The plane had left him on the beach, standing alone in the drizzle with his little pile of gear and single beat-up red surfboard. A raw wind blew ashore, slapping little grey dog-ears of chop into the wave-less cove. It was September, and the high pressure cell that he had mentioned weeks earlier had long since crept out of the Gulf and bulged into Canada, taking the last of the summer with it.

He had set up the tent in the rain and gathered what dry driftwood he could find, stuffing it under an overhang of one of the granite slabs. Shelter and fuel attended to, he set out along the beach to count the bear tracks. Grizzly bears used the beach as a highway and in past trips he often spotted them shambling towards one of the many river mouths, where they gathered in swarms to swat salmon onto the sand. This time he found no tracks. The bears had vanished, probably deep into the forest to scrounge for berries, driven by a craving for sugar after the months of living on fatty salmon flesh.

As he strode along the beach he began to feel better than he had in months. After the stale air of a city summer it refreshed him to take in great lungfuls of the chill, astringent air. He lengthened his stride, bouncing out of each deep footprint left in the sand. His sinuses cleared and as his breathing deepened he became conscious of the rise and fall of his abdomen, and he realized he had been breathing shallowly for months.

Weatherford carried no weapon and brought no radio or satellite phone. The nearest settlement was a hundred miles south or a hundred and twenty miles north, the closest hospital twice that. Aside from the sand beach, no roads existed. It would take weeks for an able–bodied man to hike out. He was completely cut off from the world. If there was an emergency with one of his patients, his staff was instructed to fax the weather station at the airfield in Russell, where Frank Colburn's air taxi service was based. He carefully briefed Colburn and left it up to him to decide whether to fly up and retrieve him. Each day at low tide – the only time a plane could safely land on the beach – Weatherford listened for the burr of the engine, convinced that the red–tailed Cessna would pop out of the gloom and dump the outside world onto him.

I thought what he did exceedingly dangerous, and offered him the EPIRB and pistol from my flying kit.

He laughed at my concern.

"Walter, I've got a wetsuit, a knife and waterproof matches. What could happen?"

He believed the bears would ignore him if he ate no meat or fish, and nothing could induce him to take pepper spray as protection.

"Can you imagine one of those canisters going off in the plane somehow?" he snorted. "Christ, you'd wish you were wading through grizzlies then."

Wilderness never purified a man, he told me, unless he had no choice but to face danger and solitude far from the lifeguard waiting to throw the buoy. What he forgot, of course, is that the wild places in summer can only be half wild – it is winter that reaps with the sharper and blacker scythe.

He awoke the first morning to a rainy and gloomy day and poked his head from the tent to check the surf. Finding the wind foul and the surf flat, he retreated back into his warm cocoon.

He stayed in the tent all day writing his cards and listening to the rain drum on the fabric of the tent. He always wrote to his patients, even those that had died, his scarcely legible script explaining treatment and, sometimes, offering apologies and even confessions. The cards he wrote to lost patients he took each year to Alaska, where he bundled them into a tin box left wedged into a cleft high up a spruce tree.

On the second morning Weatherford awoke late and listened for the sound of surf. It was still raining and the ocean sounded very still. He lay there for a long time staring up at the fat drops of rain that rolled off the tent like pearls. Presently he peeled away his sleeping bag, dressed, and unzipped the tent flaps. He knelt there for a while watching the feeble little waves scudding into the cove, barely raising a foam as they lapped at the boulders.

Disgusted, Weatherford skipped breakfast, pulled on his rubber boots, and set out hiking along the desolate shore. For miles he pressed into the bitter wind, heels kicking up a wake of black sand. Everything was cast in a leaden gray – sky, sand, sea, even the mist sailing ashore – but it was a delight to take the rain on his face and feel the cold, apple–crisp air burn down his throat. Ralph Weatherford, I think, would have found a lovely sunny day more oppressing, as his was one of those contrary souls in which beauty inflicts a terrible sadness.

On the sand, amidst the needle marks of the rain, he spied the delicate tracks of a fox, and followed them across the beach and down into the tide pools, engrossed in their story of a midnight's forage. He looked for new bear tracks, and gathered beach peas and wild greens for his lunch salad.

Browsing through the driftwood he spied a round and bright object deeply wedged between two logs. He picked up a castaway spar and pried the logs apart.

The thing fell onto the sand and beneath his feet.

It was a glass fishing float, about the size of a coconut, smooth and bottle–green, all the brighter because it was the only thing in sight that wasn't gray.

Weatherford sat heavily down upon a log, cradling the float in his lap. The rain plopped onto its surface and washed the sand from it streak by streak. He bent his head down, staring at its smooth green surface. A drop of rain found its way past his collar and traced an electric frost down his warm back. He shivered.

There had been hundreds of the glass balls at Ellen Kawena's home. They were stacked in clumps all through her careworn old Quonset hut, even spilling onto the porch and across the lawn. The floats were something of a talisman to her. Strong yet fragile, they rode the winds and waves across the ocean and somehow rarely broke when flung onto a rocky shore. In this she saw the story of her own life.

Ellen Kawena's forty-six years were not so much a life as a trajectory. She lived on the leeward side of Oahu in a rural community home to the highest percentage of native Hawaiians anywhere in the world. She had once been an Olympic swimmer, winning a silver-medal while still a student at the University of Hawaii. She went on to become the first female lifeguard in Hawaii, and in her many years on the beach gained the respect and admiration of the surfing population there. She grew to be something of a celebrity as well as a source of immense pride for the local folk. Almost pureblooded Hawaiian and determined to use her fame well, she became an activist committed to the various causes of her people.

She was diagnosed with breast cancer at forty-four. That is a bit too young, but what was strange was that she insisted a dolphin found the tumor. She swam with them nearly every day off her favorite beach, where they gathered by the hundreds, gently noodling through the calm clear waters, resting from the night's hunt. She claimed that over a period of a month a dolphin she knew by sight repeatedly sidled alongside her, rolling on its side and playfully corkscrewing around her as she swam. One day the dolphin broke from its play and shyly rubbed against her and, emitting a low, downbeat whistle, gently tapped her right breast with its muzzle.

Acting on a hunch more than superstition, Ellen went to a local clinic. A mammogram found a 7-centimeter malignant mass in her right breast. Before she could recover from the initial shock, a biopsy of one of her lymph nodes showed that the disease had already spread. That meant surgery, radiation, and then, of course, chemotherapy.

At the time Weatherford arrived in Hawaii to consult with her, she had failed two years of treatment. Two regimens of potent chemotherapeutic drugs did nothing to slow the disease and in fact it spread, infiltrating her lungs. She began to suffer respiratory seizures due to one or another obscure carcinoid syndromes and for the first time in her life Ellen was kept from the water.

She was there at the airport when Weatherford arrived, bald and frightfully frail from the ceaseless chemotherapy. When she draped the lei onto his shoulders and hugged him, he could feel how painfully thin she had become. He remembered Ellen from her pictures and, during earlier surfing trips to Hawaii, the handful of times he had seen her sitting in the lifeguard tower on one of the northern beaches. Weatherford once showed me a photograph of her in her prime. She had been a beautiful woman, tall and square–shouldered, her lean brown face set upon a neck as slender and delicate as the stem of a wine glass. In spite of his profession Weatherford was shocked at the toll the years of treatment had taken on her. If there is anything harder to look upon as the wreck of a once magnificent athlete, I suppose, it is the ruins of a once beautiful woman. Ellen had been both.

"Is it time for hospice?" she asked him the next day. She and Weatherford had spent the morning in Honolulu conferring with her oncologist. Ellen said little during the long drive home. It was barely midday but already very hot. Ellen was leading him down to the reef near her house so she could show him her 'front yard.'

"I mean, is it that bad yet?" she asked again, searching his eyes for the truth in case he was careless enough to leave it out in plain sight.

"It's not good, Ellen," he said, sidestepping the hospice question. "I won't tell you it isn't – but look, I've seen patients in far worse shape have meaningful remissions with the kind of therapy we'll be using."

They sat down in the shade of a coco palm, on a patch of sunburnt grass above the jagged lava reef. The sea breeze was rising with the heat of the day, sending chunky waves cracking onto the reef, the fine spray carrying up to them the salty tang of the tropics.

"Is it just more chemo?" she asked. "Or is it something new? I mean, my doctor didn't seem to know what you were talking about this morning."

"Well, it's a little of both, really," said Weatherford. The sun found his pale bare feet and began to redden them. He scooted deeper in to the shade "We'll use chemo, but different drugs – ones meant for other cancers – and given in a new way so they can stay in your body longer. That way, there's a better chance that they'll prevent more cancer cells from growing."

"But, Ralph, none of the other stuff worked. It just keeps spreading."

Weatherford suspected that Ellen had developed a resistance to most of the frontline chemotherapeutic drugs. Like all living organisms, cancer cells possess survival impulses and are able to mutate to defend against chemical attack. None of Ellen's scans taken during previous treatment had shown any sign of remission – in fact, her tumors seemed to harden like scar tissue to protect themselves from attack. This almost certainly indicated the presence of a multi-drug resistance. Yet, after digging through piles of abstracts from clinical trials dealing with similar cases, Weatherford was confident he could sidestep this syndrome and offer hope to Ellen.

"Yes, but this time you'll get this new combination of drugs over a longer time," he explained. "You'll have a little pump in a hip pack that'll give you the chemo in a slow infusion over five days, so the drugs remain in your blood stream longer - sort of a constant bombardment. And the nutritional support we talked about will reduce most of the side effects."

Ellen was quiet for a minute. She pulled her eyes from him and stared out to sea. It was such a lovely, sunny day out on the water.

Finally she seemed to gather her nerve. She placed a thin brown hand on his. He saw the dark purple scars of catheters and I.V. ports scattered on her forearm.

"What sort of chance do I have?"

Weatherford pictured the latest CT scans of her lungs. He hadn't told her about his suspicions of a multi-drug resistance.

"I'm hoping … I think there will be a fifty-percent chance of some remission … at least."

The sun and humidity made him drowsy. It seemed difficult for him to think and choose his words.

"Look, sometimes it takes a while to hit upon the right treatment. The good thing about this new therapy is that each of the drugs I've chosen attack the cancer in a different way – at different stages of its cellular growth. I can't promise you anything like a cure, but if we can get a remission it will buy us some time – time we can use to come up with something else."

Ellen forced a smile. She pointed to the water, changing the subject.

"Look there," she said, indicating a dark shape just beneath the surface, "That's a *honu* – a green sea turtle. They feed on the *limu* that grows on the edge of the reef."

Weatherford squinted in the bright sunshine and, spotting the turtle, watched it munch on the little stalks of seaweed as waves swung it from side to side. Ellen spoke of her life spent spearfishing along the reef, showing him the narrow chute in the lava where she entered the water. As each wave reared up a brief window opened to the shimmering reef floor. She pointed as she spied a fish, calling out its melodic Hawaiian name. Each dark patch in the reef marked a hole or ledge well known to her – she knew where every fish lived and what it ate and where it holed up at night. She once went spearfishing for her entire neighborhood but, by claiming her lungs, cancer had closed off her beloved undersea world. Yet, though it greatly distressed her to be kept from it, she was glad of the chance to show it off to a visitor.

Then the bright chatter about her spearfishing adventures ended and her mood changed.

"I don't want to end up in the hospital," she said, speaking as if in a daydream. "I want to be at home. When the time comes, I mean."

Weatherford thought, This is where I'm supposed to say 'it's not time'. He called up in his mind, like a worry stone, the abstract from the study he had chosen: *"In double-blind trials of patients with refractory end-stage metastatic breast cancer, 44% exhibited partial remission after use of Navelbine and Taxotere administered in 5-day continuous infusion..."*

When was it 'time'? thought Weatherford. When do we, as physicians, owe it to the patient to stop temporizing and begin helping them to die?

Ellen seemed to read the expression on his face.

"I'm sorry, Ralph," she said, taking his hand again and gently patting it. "It's just that no one around here will talk to me about this kind stuff. Local people feel that talking about something bad gives it too much power."

He told her that it was healthy to discuss it if she wanted to.

She drifted into deep thought again, sitting hugging her knees to her chin, chewing her lower lip.

After a while she said, "Why did this happen to me?"

"We don't know," said Weatherford, embarrassed. "Nobody does, really."

Ellen, balled up with her cheek on her knee, rocked slightly as she digested this.

"I don't want to die."

How often he had heard that – an oncologist hears it more often than does any priest. Yet Ellen said it so matter-of-factly, so stripped of the typical childlike pleading, that Weatherford was struck through a gap in his professional armor. His heart swelled with compassion for this frail but noble woman next to him, her bald head covered by a jaunty orange cap – the dying woman who had once been a lithe and powerful athlete.

A great smothering weariness settled upon him. He stammered something about the clinical trials and the hope they offered but the words clattered down with a flat counterfeit clink.

It was a long time before she could control her voice.

"What do you think it's like ... you know, to die, I mean?"

Weatherford felt sticky and unwell now. Sweat washed sunscreen into his eyes and stung them. He thought with longing of the cool Alaskan streams he drank from, of the taste of water steeped in snow and fallen spruce trees. There in Alaska, in the endless daylight of summer, nothing died but only thrived and fattened. He had never known winter there, of course.

Few patients directly ask about death – only 'when' or 'why'. We live in a culture terrified of death, hating it as ignoble failure, like losing the Big Game.

He thought it over for a moment.

"I read something once. …Someone, a writer or poet I think, said that dying was like leaving on great ship to go on a long, long voyage. You're aboard this ship, standing at the rail, waving goodbye to your friends and family on the pier. And you sail away and leave them behind, just like a trip, except that it's forever."

As soon as he said this he cringed, realizing that he had said nothing at all profound about the process of dying, that his corny platitude would scarcely comfort a child.

But Ellen looked at him thoughtfully.

"Boat Day in Honolulu," she said, brightening a little. "When I was a little girl I remember everyone would gather down at the docks in Honolulu to watch the ships leave. All these people were there to see their friends or family off. Everybody cried: the people on the ship because they were leaving Hawaii, going back to the snow and jobs and troubles. And everyone on the dock cried because it was such a long voyage and the rest of the world seemed so far away and scary to them. It was sad, I tell you. Even folks that had no one to see off came down to the harbor if they needed a good cry."

Weatherford watched her, silent. He pictured the throng of well-wishers on the dock, the passengers crowding the rail, the lei thrown in the wake as the ship steamed off into the limitless, eternal sea.

'Everybody keeps telling me we go to a 'better place'," Ellen sighed. "I'm sick of hearing it." She swept a hand, indicating the world before them: the fish glittering beneath the waves, the rich black lava rock aflame with red and green seaweed, the palm fronds whispering back to the sea breeze. "You see, I don't want to go anywhere else."

Weatherford saw that while her eyes were shiny, no tears would come. Chemotherapy, in parching the mucous membranes, stole her ability to shed tears. She looked away, gripping fistfuls of grass as she struggled to control her feelings.

"Where. ...Where could be better than this?" she said finally, and her voice held no bitterness and only love.

Weatherford sat in the rain on the wild nameless beach, staring at the glass float in his lap. The raindrops smacking down on the glass might have been his tears. Yet, as he once admitted to me, he never wept. Cancer, too, had robbed him, as it had Ellen, of the ability to shed tears. There remained only a hollow numbness, an emptiness that frightened him like the sudden loss of one of his senses. This often happens when a physician confronts a tough case away from a clinical setting. Very early in one's career the oncologist learns that acute empathy can be just as corrosive to one's soul as callous indifference.

He stood and looked back in the direction of his camp. More rain was coming. A squall line was visible to the south, the rain slanting in great arching combs over the metallic sea. It would be another day without a fire. The thought of spending the day mewed up inside the tent repulsed him. If he was to be wet and miserable he might as well go surfing.

He gently set the glass float on the sand and turned towards the camp – in Alaska he allowed himself nothing he found there – but changed his mind and picked it up again. Stuffing it into his parka, he followed his tracks back to the tent.

It took him half an hour to suit up. His wetsuit lay on a granite slab by the tent, sodden and cold. He nerved himself to strip and wriggle into it, hopping on one foot atop the slab, breath sucked out of him as the chilled wetsuit touched his chest. Next he pulled on thick neoprene boots, gasping as his warm toes squished into them. Then came the earplugs, covered by a black rubber hood. Now sealed from head to toe, he donned the bulky neoprene mitts that turned his hands into clumsy lobster claws.

Weatherford picked up his surfboard and walked north along the beach, growing warmer as his body heat simmered against the thick skin of neoprene, bringing the clammy, womblike warmth he'd long since learned to crave.

He trudged a mile down the beach before he found surf large enough to interest him. There, a large creek dumped into the sea, creating a shoaling comma of sand that pulled in and amplified the little swells, sending them curling down its length with good form, if not size.

He was bored with the surf after fifteen minutes. He stayed out anyway. It didn't matter. It was the raw conditions that excited him, the frontiersman's sense of awe at his surroundings. The rain felt sharper here than in the South, the winds fiercer, the seawater preternaturally colder. He imagined himself on another planet, where the mountains towered up in shapes dictated by an alien logic, their peaks bulwarked by a bear–haunted forest guarded by enormous eagles that sat sentry–like atop the towering palisades of spruce.

A feeling of well–being settled upon Weatherford. Bobbing off this wild shore, his thoughts drifted into a favorite mental hobby of thinking about retiring from his practice. He entered into contemplation of retirement as a model railway builder climbed down into his basement workshop. It was a pleasant pastime for him to painstakingly construct a life of simple, quiet order. He once told me that he frequently thought about moving to Alaska. An experienced physician, he mused, would be welcome in a remote town on the Alaskan coast. He would be seen as an eccentric – a surfing doctor, another kooky pilgrim from Outside – but certainly the locals would be grateful to have a resident practitioner. But what about winter? Would he tolerate the ceaseless rain and cold and scant five hours of murky daylight? Would it be worth it, he wondered, to be free of oncology, to have a small office where he could attend to flesh and bone mangled not by malignancy but by chainsaws and trawler winches.

As he sat there thinking, letting the little waves roll past him, the wind veered to the west and the rain thinned to a light drizzle. Higher up, the seamless cloud mass rolled into the mountains, foaming like surf against the reef of unseen peaks. To the southwest, he noticed a band of blue–gray light squatting low on the horizon. The rain might let up soon. Weatherford had skipped breakfast and was suddenly very hungry. If the weather cleared, he could have a hot meal, perhaps even a fire. He caught the next wave that came in and, not bothering to stand up, rode it to shore prone.

By the time he made it back to camp the rain had stopped. A pearly gray overcast flooded everything with light. He stood transfixed, eyes watering in the sudden brightness, marveling at the inexhaustible range of gray tones that comprise the Alaskan palette.

He peeled off his wetsuit and pulled on his damp clothes. Then, feeling damper and colder than he had in his wetsuit, he found the hatchet and cracked the driest chunk of firewood into lengths of kindling. After an hour of coaxing and fussing over the damp splinters, he gave up and soaked the whole mess with white gas from his cook stove. As the fire came grudgingly to life, he stacked more wood next to the fire pit to dry, and cooked his lunch.

He sat with his back to the fire, wet parka steaming as it dried, burning his tongue on a mug of scalding miso broth. A block of heated granite, rolled from the fire pit, warmed his bare feet. He leaned over occasionally to stir the pot of curried potatoes bubbling on the cook stove. Beneath the sounds of crackling flame and the cooking food came the gentle music of the dripping forest. Weatherford drifted into drowsy contentment.

He sat there all afternoon, poking at the fire, watching the tide rise and fill the little cove, thinking over the treatments he might fall back on if Ellen Kawena failed her latest chemotherapy.

A line of birds materialized to the north, flying towards his campsite in a wavering V formation. He gazed absently at them as they passed overhead, the furious rustle of wings sounding like a tiny storm of dry leaves. A few minutes later another group of birds appeared above the same rocky headland a couple of miles to the north. Again they passed overhead, low enough to clearly see their eyes. Some of the birds gazed incuriously down at him but most, upon rounding the point, expectantly searched ahead for their next landfall. Probably navigating from point to point, thought Weatherford, now making for Cape Fairmount, the next point south. …South! It dawned on him that for the whole of his trip he had not seen a single bird flying north.

Another formation wheeled over his campsite and he imagined he saw on their faces the terrified grimace of animals fleeing a predator. Winter! Winter was coming. For a moment their blind animal panic seized him, overwhelming him with a sudden dread of being left behind as winter lurched down from its terrible netherworld.

Then it was dusk, long before he expected it. How great was the difference between summer and autumn in the North! For the first time in all his travels there he felt uneasy.

Weatherford slept fitfully that night. The air was clammy and very still and he had to peel down half of his sleeping bag. Overhead, the clouds drifted beneath a pale sliver of moon, the stars described their polar orbs, but without the lullaby of the rain, sleep evaded him. Finally he slept, slipping immediately into the cocoon–like dream state of the solitary camper.

He dreamt he was standing in a sunny green meadow overlooking the sea. Ellen

Kawena stood next to him, healthy and square shouldered, her rich brown hair gleaming in the sunlight. It was a beautiful day, the ocean a sparkling clear blue. Ellen was getting ready to go diving, chirping like a bird delighted at an early spring.

"Oh, Ralph, look how the sand in the channel glows! The water is so clear!"

But he was distracted and wasn't listening. The air was cool and fresh, with the scent of pine, like northern California, yet the ocean was unmistakably tropical. He wanted to share her joy but felt only confusion and dread.

"I bet there's choke fish under the ledge today," she laughed, rubbing toothpaste on the faceplate of her dive mask. "Ten-point days like this we say, 'Ho, start the hibachi, already.' I'll get one full bag in no time!"

Scarcely listening, he turned his head to catch a far-away sound. Somewhere in the distance a conch shell blew. Its solemn, wavering lilt caught him in the throat and

suddenly he knew what he could not have
known.

He turned to Ellen.

"It's time, Ellen. We should go."

She ignored him, singing happily to herself
as she rubbed wax onto the shaft of her three-
prong spear.

He put his hand on her shoulder.

"Ellen, we should go. We'll be late. They're
waiting."

She said nothing, and continued to fuss
with her gear as if he wasn't there.

"Ellen…"

She flashed a look of irritation at him, like
a little girl interrupted in play by a scolding
parent.

"I don't know what you're talking about."

"It's … it's for you. They're all waiting for
you."

She tossed her head toward the sound of
the trumpeting conch shell.

"It's okay, Ralph," she shrugged. "It's all for them, anyway. They'll be fine."

She bent down and put on her swim fins, pulled the mask over her face, and, without another word duck–walked to the water's edge. As she slid beneath the surface he saw her hair spread out in a thick brown fan, saw her spear quiver as she pulled back the rubber sling, and heard her silver laughter echo strangely in her snorkel as she pointed her fins skyward and dove for the reef below.

It was oddly calm when Weatherford awoke in the morning. The air in the tent, made stale and sour by his wet boots and socks, had given him a splitting headache. He unzipped the tent, pulled on his parka and boots, and crunched over the gravel to his lookout post atop the granite slab.

Masses of broken cloud scudded beneath a ceiling of rusty overcast – it was another deliciously rotten day. Pockets of mist seeped from the forest and sailed along the beach. And the surf had risen overnight – though still small, the swells were noticeably thicker and more evenly spaced. Weatherford sat down on the edge of the slab to watch. With luck the surf would probably pick up with the incoming tide later that afternoon. But the prospect of good surf couldn't submerge his strange and vivid dream, so he sat staring at the leaden sea, haunted by what he remembered.

Ellen, healthy and bright, tugging on her fins.

Ellen, slipping into the warm calm sea, her laughter ringing out as she glided toward the waiting reef.

Happily swallowed up by the sea – what a contrast that was to the realities of end–stage disease: The accelerating cascade of complications, the oxygen cannula, the meals pushed away untasted in the sterile hospital room, the battery of medications. It was always hard for him to preside over that final sea–

change, when a person he had fought for wasted into a thin husk.

'Sea–change' -- once he actually had been that philosophical about it!

'Nothing of him that doth fade

But hath suffered a sea-change

Into something rich and strange.'

Shakespeare and chemotherapy! Why not garlic and crucifixes? As if cancer was merely a clarifying storm one had to pass through to reach 'the opposite shore'. If he hadn't interfered Ellen would now be in Texas, treated according to the conventional playbook, some other doctor's responsibility. She trusted him to make for her the most important decision of her life. What if he was wrong?

Weatherford sat on the rock for a long time watching the tide go out.

The plane appeared an hour later.

He was bending over the cook stove stirring a pot of oatmeal when he detected the faint burr of the engine. He hurried up onto the rocks and scoured the southern skyline. Perhaps it wasn't Colburn, just someone heading up to the Dangerous River for the last fishing of the season. Then he spotted the little single–engine plane beetling along over the beach and he knew it was Colburn.

What emergency would bring him out two days early? Weatherford's pulse quickened as he sifted through his current patients. None of them were in danger of a 'crash dive,' none were at any crucial stage of treatment – except for Ellen, and she was safely under the supervision of another physician.

The plane flew overhead and banked over the forest. He saw Colburn crane his head sideways, looking for obstructions on the sand. Weatherford turned off the stove and rushed down the point as Colburn flung the machine around in a wide arc, straightened into a short approach, and set down on the sand a hundred yards from the base of the point. Weatherford waited at the edge of the sand, anxious and out of breath from his sprint over the rocky shore, as the plane waddled toward him, its big beach tires bouncing over clumps of kelp.

The engine sputtered and died. Weatherford stooped under the wing and pulled open the right-side door.

"Hi, ya, Doc," Colburn said, taking off his headset. "Sorry to barge in on you so early like."

"What's the matter?"

"Storm coming. Remember that low we were looking at, the one that was supposed to traipse on up into the Bering Sea?"

"Yeah?"

"Well, it didn't. Moved on over to Kodiak, instead. Turned into one hell of a pit, too. Figured I better grab you right away or you might be stuck here 'till April."

Weather! That's all, thank God, thought Weatherford, just weather.

He laughed, relieved that it was not a patient. "And the surf was just coming up!"

"Well, it'll be coming up a whole lot more real soon," said Colburn with a grim smile. "This sucker's packing a wallop."

"Seems calm enough here...."

"Yeah, but not for long. Up top you can already see the front down the coast a ways. Whole southern horizon is black. Look," Colburn continued, all business now, "how fast can you pack up? We should get going – we've gotta make it back to Russell before that front hits or we'll be hiking this machine out on our backs."

"Give me half an hour. How's that?"

"Sure, Doc. ...And can you manage on your own? Good, I'd like to have some breakfast," Colburn said, extracting a Thermos and an enormous sandwich from a paper sack on his lap. "Been up since five without a bite. Had to pull out some hunters over by Twelvemile Lake."

It took Weatherford an hour to break camp. He insisted on leaving behind no imprint of his visit. He scattered the rocks of the fire pit, and buried the ash deep in the sand. The logs that had been his chairs and tables he dragged askew, as if the hand of nature had placed them so. When at last the tent and sleeping bag were bundled into a large duffel bag he climbed up on the tallest granite boulder and looked to the south. A mass of black cloud, oiling northward like a sinister dark glacier, blotted out the southwestern horizon. Alarmed, he jumped down and set to packing with renewed urgency.

Colburn stuffed the last morsel of sandwich into his mouth as Weatherford returned stumbling and sweating under the weight of his baggage.

"Oh, almost forgot," Colburn said, still chewing. He wiped his greasy hands on his Synchilla vest and handed Weatherford a plain white envelope. "Fax came through for you at the weather station."

Weatherford tore open the envelope. Inside was a sheet of physician's stationery with a single typewritten paragraph. Colburn saw the color drain from Weatherford's wind–burnt face.

"Bad news?" asked the pilot.

Weatherford stared absently at the few lines now blurring on the page.

"Yes..." he mumbled. "Very bad. ...A patient of mine."

It was all there in the oncologist's spare, sterile note. *"The patient, Ellen Kawena, Stage 4 infiltrating ductile carcinoma ... Seemed to tolerate the first cycle of drugs ... white blood cell count fell below the line during nadir ... temperature climbed to 104 degrees ... admitted to hospital ... pneumonia ... consciousness lost ... expired in the early hours of the morning."*

It was a fate so common as to be unremarkable.

"Sorry to hear it, Doc," said Colburn. He paused. "Look, we better get moving. The wind's kicking up already..."

Weatherford turned and looked seaward. The tossing seas were bigger now and very white against the blackening sky. A few fat drops of water tapped then splattered the paper he held in his hand. He gently folded the note into a small square and tucked it into his pocket. Then they both climbed into the cockpit as the clouds broke apart and rain drummed with a fury upon the plane.

"Sitka just closed down," said Colburn, fiddling with the volume of his radio headset. They had been aloft for about 45 minutes, heading southeast. "Juneau's got southeast winds at 24 knots, gusting to 35. Won't be anyone getting in there soon."

Weatherford nodded but made no reply. He peered down at the narrowing strip of black beach scrolling by. There was a crosswind component now as the wind veered to the south–southwest, sending the plane crabbing along the coast. They pierced a curtain of rain and for a moment all was dark – nothing but the clatter of rain on metal, the howl of the propeller, and the little bowls of light scooped from the murk by the running lights on the wingtips. Colburn tipped the nose down to stay beneath the lowering ceiling, stung with a miserly bitterness at having to dole out another 50 feet.

Weatherford glanced at the altimeter. 750 feet.

It was darker now. The sand and sea and wet forest were so black they absorbed what little daylight remained. Colburn flipped a switch and the cabin glowed in the soft orange lights of the instrument panel.

The plane emerged from the belt of rain and Weatherford anxiously looked down at the sea. The wind was blowing harder now and they crawled against it so slowly that he could watch individual whitecaps rise and topple and rise again.

"Shee–it!" said Colburn with a nervous laugh. "Ever see a sky like that down South?"

But there no longer seemed to be any sky, no horizon. All that remained was an edgeless canopy of seamless cloud, purple and black like the underside of a venomous mushroom.

The beach narrowed as the coast trended west into a sickle-shaped headland. The gap between the breakers and the driftwood wall shrank to 40 or 50 feet. A few miles ahead the coast disappeared into a misty blur. Weatherford squinted, trying to follow the shore beyond the veil of … was it fog? Or another squall line?

Colburn glanced at the folded square of map on the clipboard strapped to his knee.

"Well, this is the end of the sand here. The coast is all broken up and rocky from here on, remember?"

"Yes. Is that fog?" asked Weatherford.

"Dunno. Probably. The mountains are closer to the coast here and there's a fair bit of ice inland." The pilot paused, drumming his knee, thinking. "Whatever the hell it is, we probably can't see in it."

At 750 feet, they were at the bare minimum he thought safe. The ceiling would likely only lower ahead if it didn't clamp all the way down and soon, even in the worst emergency, they would have no place to land. Frank Colburn had seen too many pilots fly into eternity pushing it to get home. It was madness to go on. Before he could make up his mind instinct commanded his foot to ease down on the right rudder pedal. A slight turn of the yoke, and they were banking into a long, shallow right turn back out over the sea. The aircraft shook as they pulled away from the wind. The right wing tilted so that Weatherford looked straight down at the saw-toothed breakers.

Then the wings leveled and they were headed back against their original course. The wind, now crosswind on their tail, sent the plane lurching into shuddering drops. Startled, Weatherford cinched his harness tight. Each sudden plunge sent his head bumping into the cockpit roof. The aircraft suddenly seemed to him very small and fragile. There was still a half a mile of visibility but he was aware that the ceiling could crash down to the deck at any moment. With the sand beneath them, they were safe for the moment – but the tide was moving in fast.

Now the slender strip of sand offering safety dissolved into a curtain of rain.

Colburn clucked his tongue.

"Keep your eye on the beach, Doc," he said. "Look for any place clear enough to land, I don't care if it's the size of a tennis court. I'll turn upwind when you say when."

A forced landing in Alaska! Weatherford's scalp prickled as adrenalin swept through him. His heart pounding, he turned to look down, fumbling to loosen his harness so he could lean closer to the window. Colburn glanced at his passenger. He could see Weatherford's drawn and colorless face reflected in the window.

"Don't worry – it might be a little bumpy, but at least we'll be on the ground."

Weatherford nodded, keeping his eyes trained on the line of sand scrolling by. His pulse thundered in his ears. The treetops streaked by in a green blur. The rain blackened everything. In the murky light it was impossible to clearly discern the wet sand from the piled driftwood. The waves looked higher now. Already whitewater was licking over the main berm and would soon spill into the low gully between it and the forest.

Colburn's finger tapped nervously on the yoke. He sneaked a glance at the map fixed to the little clipboard strapped to his knee.

"Think I've got a better idea, Doc. Look..." he said, unclipping the map and handing it to Weatherford.

Ten miles north a shallow river valley lay between a wide, low part in the mountains, leading to a glacial basin that climbed to a narrow mountain pass. The local bush pilots used the Chiltka Gap as a shortcut in the summer, though even then only in immaculate weather. If Colburn could somehow squeeze through the Gap they would gain the sheltered inner waters of Chiltka Sound – only 60 miles NNW of the Russell airstrip.

"There'll be nowhere to put down if the engine packs up," explained Colburn. "But I think we may have a higher ceiling in there away from the coast."

"Have you flown that way before?" asked Weatherford.

"Yeah, plenty in clear weather. I know the route." He paused to adjust the rudder trim. "Like I said, the weather's different in there, especially around them glaciers. Sometimes better, sometimes worse – but if it's rotten in there I suppose we can turn around and come back out here to the coast and hope there's still some dry sand around."

How like the abstract of a clinical trial study it sounded, Weatherford thought wryly. In a moment of clairvoyant vision he pictured the tiny column buried on page 5 of the newspaper:

"Small Plane Missing." Another aircraft lost in Alaska. Another plane sawn into pieces by mountains that weren't supposed to be there, another clump of metal swallowed unseen into waiting crevasses and slowly digested by the prehistoric glaciers.

Ahead, hovering in the mist, was a wide muddy river mouth cleaving the forest and cutting across the beach.

"This is it – we gotta' decide," said Colburn.

Weatherford again strained to make out detail on the beach. Using the storm winds to reduce their groundspeed, Colburn could certainly land on a scrap of open sand. Yet the storm would soon swamp the beach – the bigger winter storms swept deep into the forest. The plane would be lost. Possibly they might taxi along the shore and with luck find a breach in the endless pile of drift logs into which they could tuck the plane – but there would have to be a corresponding gap in the wall of trees.

"Alright," said Weatherford, his throat tight. "Let's try your shortcut."

Colburn nodded. As he started the turn into the river valley he was already transmitting their new flight plan and position to the control center in Anchorage.

It was darker over the river. Among the wet black trees and muddy grey water there was only a soupy twilight. The wide coastal delta soon pinched into a valley that after a few miles angled suddenly to the southeast. Colburn clung to the right-hand bank, creeping around each bend with just a touch of rudder. Weatherford searched for a place they could land in an emergency - sandspit, gravel bar, anything - but was appalled to find only the nervous dark river foaming over rocks and root-torn trees. A man would have a hard time finding a firm footing much less set down an airplane.

Colburn, glancing at him, seemed to read his mind.

"Pretty spooky in here, eh?" he said mildly. "I've seen worse. But the visibility's already a bit better. Beats eating M.R.E.s and Pop-Tarts in the rain for three days."

Weatherford gratefully lapped up the pilot's confidence. The patient in the examining room, the passenger in a stricken plane - each look for hope in the carefully vague prognosis handed them. Relaxing somewhat, he remembered the little square of paper in his pocket. He had told Ellen that there was hope, had turned her mind away from preparing for death. She would have preferred to face it head-on. He thought of the little faded house now empty, its treasures gathering dust. He thought of the sunny reef, now unloved; of Ellen, the champion swimmer drowned in her own flooded lungs.

The plane shuddered as a gust got a hold of it. Weatherford surfaced from his reverie and turned anxiously to Colburn.

"Katabatic wind," soothed the pilot. "Always kinda' squirrelly in here. Just think of it like potholes on a road."

They flew into another bend as the valley hooked back to the east. Its flanks were steeper now and furrowed with streaks of ice. Scrawny trees sprouted from cracks of soil, and the plane flew so close to them that Weatherford saw that their flailing branches had scraped ovals of bare rock from the ice. He shot a nervous look at Colburn.

"Why are we so close to the side?"

The pilot made no reply for a few moments.

"More room this way," he said, distracted. "More room to turn around in a hurry."

Then he nudged the rudder and they wheeled along the valley wall as it again curved to the south, the Cessna jolting at each burst of wind.

They flew on in silence for half an hour, each awestruck by the desolate country and the urgency wrought by even the slightest change in weather. The steady drone of the engine, the rocking plane, the warm cabin – all conspired to swamp Weatherford's mind with a drowsy fear. Everything depended on the ceiling: The clouds must not drop any lower.

The terrain began to rise. They climbed with it, until Colburn trimmed out just beneath the roof of cloud, so that it seemed as if they were skimming, inverted, the surface of a midnight sea. The ground rose, their anxiety with it, and then fell away again. The river broke into rapids and just as abruptly broadened into a sluggish marsh. Then the banks flattened, the valley walls fell away, and they were flying over a great mudflat. Soon they were at the edge of a shallow silvery lake, littered with chunks of ice and denuded logs. Colburn checked his heading to the map and turned to skirt the southern edge of the lake.

Weatherford peered down at the grim world scrolling by. This was a new and horrible country to him, a vast glacial wasteland crushed by ice and flooded by melt water, where no living thing planted root or claw. A feeling of unquenchable loneliness crept over him, as if he were marooned on an airless cold asteroid far from the dim blue glow of Earth.

Colburn turned to dodge a rainsquall that hung across the lake. Edging around it to the south they skimmed over mile after mile of mud and reeds. When they turned back on course the lake was gone, replaced by a leprous skin of broken and earth-stained ice. Everywhere, as far as they could see in the dim light, splintered chunks of rotting brown ice tilted and sagged.

Gaping at the dreadful void scrolling beneath him, Weatherford suddenly knew that he was drawn to the wilderness because there, in the desolate places, he could explore fear and death with little risk, as people do by watching horror movies. Perhaps he went there because he desperately needed to confront death in places where it existed only in its most primeval form. Places too elemental and raw for disease to take root.

But now, suspended over this terrible nothingness, he wanted only to get safely across it. Somewhere off in the gray mist awaited the lamp-lit world of man – the little airstrip at Russell, the lodge where awaited clean warm clothes and a gas-heated shower, the snug diner with its fresh hot food. He contemplated of all this, agonizing with the physician's sharp acuity over the countless things had to go exactly right before that world could again be reached. Air, he thought, must continue to rush over the wings at just the right speed and angle. Millions of precisely measured spurts of fuel must explode in perfect rhythm within the cylinders. …And the clouds must not sink any lower.

They flew on without speaking, east by southeast, until a line of mountains filled the windscreen. Then the ice field was behind them, and they were climbing with the rising ceiling over talus that sloped up toward a saddle between two steeple-topped mountains – the Chiltka Gap. The aircraft shook in the wind pouring down the basin, though scarcely noticed by Weatherford, whose senses were tingling in awareness of the narrowing terrain.

A rainsquall sailed into their path just as they were poised to shoot between the two peaks. Colburn hesitated, and then decided to go on. If visibility worsened he would have a few minutes to turn back. Farther on, he knew, the Gap narrowed and there would be no room to complete a turn. The plane poked hesitantly into the squall, rain rattling on the wings and fuselage like gravel. The ground rushed beneath in a blur of rock and ice. Rain smothered the windshield, the frantic wipers scraping it away in curling streamers that exploded into mist past the side windows. Colburn cursed his decision to go on. No margin of safety remained. They were taking an appalling risk. A part of him seemed to detach and hover over himself, scolding, "This is how it happens." He glanced at the temperature gauge. His heart sank. It was growing colder outside. There was a danger of ice forming on the plane. Absently humming some nameless tune, he scribbled their position on a scrap of paper. A fine dew of sweat appeared on his temples. If they took ice he would have to declare an emergency and do his best to set down somewhere in the Gap.

He stole a look at the port wing. There it was – ice – creeping in a pearly glaze over the black strip on the leading edge of the wing.

He tried to swallow, but his throat was dry. If the ice continued to accumulate, it would be a matter of minutes before the wings would lose most of their lift. Any second now, perhaps, the nose would drop and the yoke would turn to mush. He added throttle and lowered the nose as much as he dared. It was too dangerous to risk a turn – better to pour on the coal and keep level and trim, anything but induce a stall.

Colburn anxiously eyed the ground below. He made up his mind – the second he sensed the elevators getting heavy he would pancake onto the nearest bit of level ground. Anything was better than flying into the side of a mountain or falling out of the sky in a stall.

...But, by God, how he wished the Cessna had retractable gear! It would be a miracle if he could keep the aircraft from somersaulting over the uneven terrain.

The pilot cinched his harness tight and instructed Weatherford to do the same. Nothing to do to but send the emergency call...

"Anchorage Center, this is Cessna Three–One–Six–Zero–Zulu.... Uh..."

Then the clatter of rain ceased and they were through it. The low clouds gave way, replaced by a raised ceiling of dull black overcast. Below a wide calm inlet materialized beneath them, inky black and stretching east into an enormous bay. This was the leeward side of the coastal mountains – the Chiltka Gap was behind them.

The wipers squeaked on dry glass. Colburn switched them off. With a trembling hand, he reset the altimeter to match the barometer at Russell. He stole a glance at Weatherford but the doctor was staring down in astonishment at the placid inlet, his bloodless hands gripping the seat.

"Some good hunting down there," said the pilot, trying to sound the unflappable bush pilot. "Fella' took a record mountain sheep out of here a few years back."

Weatherford, unsure of his voice, could only nod. He was suddenly very tired. Home was still days away. When the storm passed there would be another flight to Juneau, and another to San Francisco. Strange – it would still be summer there.

The propeller droned its soothing song, and he dozed loose-necked in his harness.

It began to rain again but the ceiling was higher now and the plane bored along trim and level at 1100 feet. Colburn nudged the doctor awake and, smiling broadly, tilted the plane on its side so that Weatherford could see below. There was a glimpse of dirt road, a truck crawling through the rain, a corrugated shack beside a lake.

Ahead a revolving beacon flailed through the mist.

"Russell below, Doc," said Colburn. "Everybody's gone for the winter but the lights come on automatically."

Winter. It came to all places eventually, reflected Weatherford, even to Hawaii. He thought of Ellen Kawena, of the letter he would write to her and, next spring, place in the little box he left in the tree below Mount Foraker.

The green runway lamps flickered to life as they swooped into the base leg. The pilot cut the power and the plane sank toward the earth. For a moment there was no sound but the drumming rain and the wind whistling through the struts.

Weatherford tried to imagine Ellen gone but couldn't. Yet it occurred to him that it was impossible to picture her cured, either. She wouldn't have wanted him to remember her withered and sick. No, he decided, he would write to the whole and vital women he had visited in his dream.

The fat tires bounced onto the runway. The rain turned to sleet and the sleet became floating flakes of snow. As silently as death, winter pressed down on the North.

Relics

Some people say that there are things that you cannot take out of Hawaii. Indeed, the ancients devised the *kapu* system to keep the spiritual power, or *mana*, of a sacred object from being contaminated by lesser people or things. This is a story of one such object – a surfboard – that was removed from and then returned to Hawaii.

It happened that there was an enormous auction for antique surfboards in Honolulu and collectors from all over the world came to appraise, covet, and perhaps bid on many old and valuable surfboards. Many of these boards could easily be dated back fifty years. One surfboard in particular was much, much older.

The wealthy man's auction strives to be a dignified and stately affair, but the chewed fingernails, dew of sweat about the temples, and the stale dry mouths betray the forced dignity of the occasion. The billion–dollar surfing industry had created its own *nouveau riche* class, and here they were with florid sunburned faces and one hundred and fifty dollar aloha shirts draped over an office paunch, yelling into cell phones and warring with one another for some touchstone of their youth to hang like a trophy on the wall at home.

Yet in spite of all this wealth the most exclusive station at the auction was not in the VIP rows of the packed auditorium but was in fact outside, back behind the cafeteria where a group of aging pioneer surfers – some Hawaiian, some *haole,* and some unsure – had found a picnic table hidden away behind the dumpsters. In this quiet corner they sat in the cool evening breeze to drink beer from a battered old ice chest and "talk story."

After a few beers they began to uncoil from the strain of the pre–auction party. None of them were comfortable at these big gatherings that their friend 'Dozer Larson railroaded them into.

"Damn, I was so glad 'Dozer didn't make me get up and make a speech or some goddammed thing," said Walt Schaefer. Walt was a surfboard shaper who had built his first board in 1951, and many of his old balsawood boards were held in such esteem that a number of them could be said to comprise the centerpiece of the auction that evening.

"Ho, me too. I never like talk," agreed Sully Ho'olehua. The famed Hawaiian surfer who had ruled Waikiki for a generation shouldered his diplomatic chores with dignity, but he was relieved to be outside and safely hidden from the fray. "My jaw stay sore from fake smiling."

"Frickin' 'Dozer," grumbled Clayton Kanahele, wiping a smear of barbeque sauce from his chin as he attacked the last of a plate of shortribs. "Told me it was going to be one sit down dinner, not one stand up *pupu* party. How you going to stand and eat ribs and shake hands all at the same time? I'm still hungry. Hey, Kimo, how about you sneak around front and grab us some more ribs?"

Kimo Harrington was the youngest of them and the only one who still actively surfed. He was the little *hapa* kid that the older guys had adopted as their mascot back in the early '60s.

"No way, bruddah," Kimo replied, "I 'aint going back in there. There's this one *haole* guy keeps asking me to sign his frickin' shirt."

Clayton turned to regard his friend Kaleo Akana, a quiet and shy Hawaiian who sat off to the side absent-mindedly tuning his guitar to slack key. He was beaming with the joy of being with his old compatriots but more than content to listen from the sidelines. Kaleo lived way out on the windward side where he took care of his elderly mother. He didn't get out much anymore.

"Kaleo, you like get bruddah Clayton some grinds?"

"Shoots," he agreed, but didn't move. He just sat there with his lopsided smile, tilting an ear towards the liquid strums he produced on the guitar.

Clayton shrugged and turned back to the others.

"Sheez, 'Dozer came all *momona* the last couple years." He was splattered with barbeque sauce and rather stout himself.

"Well, he's successful now," said Walt. He drained his can of beer and tossed it into the dumpster. Sully popped open a fresh can and handed it to him. "The buggah's been plugging away in the surfboard business all these years, never two dimes to rub together and, wham, he starts a clothing line, all that retro crap comes back in – the Japanese go nuts over it – and now he's chomping a cigar and bossing us around."

Over the last few years 'Dozer had been herding the old gang around to conventions, tournaments and tradeshows. They were all famous and respected watermen – billed as "surf legends" – and though they felt at times as if they were prodded about like cigar store Indians at these gatherings, they didn't really begrudge Larson. It was worth it all to get together and drink and shoot the breeze.

"I don't mind," Kimo shrugged, "This is good fun, eh? And bruddah 'Dozer pays for everything"

"Here's to 'Dozer," said Sully, holding up his beer, "Hooray for 'Dozer…."

They all chimed in with the infamous toast from the old days:

"Hoo-ray for 'Dozer,

Hoo-ray at last.

Hoo-ray for 'Dozer,

He's a horse's ass.

He's a ho-oorse's okole!"

The backdoor to the auditorium sprang open and the frenzy of the crowd inside roared out to them. 'Dozer himself appeared, red–faced and sweating, and cried, "I heard that you guys!

Hey, Walt, some *ass*hole just paid eleven grand for one of your crappy old balsas."

"Ho, Walt, who'd a thought, bruddah?" said Clayton, "You should have kept some of those old slabs. Shoots, *I* should have kept some. Remember that redwood–balsa spear you made me for Sunset?" He whistled appreciatively. "That board was magic. You was living in that rusty old Quonset hut, living on peanut butter and stolen pineapples."

"...And that little *hapa*-Filipino girl from Wahiawa," added Kimo.

Sully nodded and laughed, "Yeah, and you went use the pineapples for make *swipe* one time, because I remember we all had for take one turn sawing out that sucking board. Had one hangover and got seasick standing on top the blank with that big old saw making the sawhorses wobble all over."

Everyone laughed. Kaleo giggled quietly to himself. It had been a while since they had been able to sit down like this, to drink and shoot the breeze without autograph seekers or nostalgia buffs sticking coffee table books in their faces and asking them *do you remember that wave, huh? Huh? … and wasn't that a '65 Brewer gun with the reverse-lap Volan? Do you know how much that board is* worth *today?*

Walt wasn't laughing. He picked angrily at some splinters on the edge of the table.

"Goddam collectors," he spat, "I can't even afford one of my own boards. How's that? And they've made 'em too frickin' valuable to even ride anymore. You know the bastard will probably hang it on a wall somewhere."

"Stop grumbling already. You never could shape worth beans," joked Sully, "You're lucky anybody even like pay that much money for one of those old piece–a–shit boards."

"Hey, it just sucks," Walt said, ruffled now. He had been having a hard time lately. The surfboard cottage industry, which he'd had a hand in almost from the beginning, was all in a shambles. The new computer-controlled shaping machines and overseas molded boards were changing everything, taking work away from the guys that got up every morning and drew out a planshape on a blank and talked to a customer about where he surfed and how he stood on a board. He could go and make wall–hangers for this booming nostalgia market, but he swore that he'd fall back onto his contractor's license before resorting to that. *Surfboards have* mana, he thought, *go ahead and ride those soulless pop-outs. Made in Thailand! Well, at least in thirty years there won't be any of these frickin' auctions with* haole-*feet yuppies squabbling over some stamped-out kook model.*

"Ah, to hell with it," he shrugged, "Let 'em take it. Just means there'll be one more board on a wall, one less kook in the water."

Everyone was quiet for a time. They'd heard that Walt had been getting a reputation as a crusty old grump. But they were all safely cashiered out of the surfing industry; they played golf, worked in the yard, went fishing, spoiled their grandkids. Walt Schaefer was still in it though times had changed.

It was dusk now. An orchestra of birds fussed over their evening refuge in the banyan trees. The tradewinds found their way through the high rises and brought the soft cool air down from the Ko'olaus. Time, as it will during the Hawaiian twilight, slowed to a crawl and then seemed to stop. Sully belched, stood up and opened the cooler he had been seated upon, casting a judicious eye on the supply. Good. There was plenty for the rest of the evening. He pulled another brace of bottles from the ice.

Once again the backdoor to the auditorium was flung open. 'Dozer emerged in a tumult of wild cheers carrying an enormous balsawood surfboard. Behind him they had a brief glimpse of the sea of flushed, excited faces that were just turning away from Larson and back towards the auctioneer as he called their attention to the next sale.

Then the door was shut and it was calm once more. 'Dozer, looking pop-eyed and a bit breathless, hefted the balsa board onto an empty picnic table.

"Jesus, it's crazy in there," he said, wiping the sweat from his eyes.

"Hey, isn't that one of your old shapes?" asked Kimo.

"Yeah, but it sure felt lighter forty years ago."

Walt smirked. "What did you do, Larson, buy one of your own boards?"

"Hell no, I just need you guys to sign this thing for me," he replied, brandishing a fat black marking pen.

This was all part of the job. They obediently lined up to sign the board, Sully in careful neat printing near the nose, Clayton beneath him with an indifferent scrawl. Clayton handed the pen to Walt.

Walt bent down to sign, but stopped and looked side-eye at 'Dozer.

"Hey, wait a minute – is this going to be hung in some lawyer's office, or what?"

Larson sat down gratefully, a sigh hissing through his teeth. "Just sign it, alright? It's going to the Hale'iwa Surf Museum, okay? They squeezed their donation box so they could have this board. At least it'll stay in Hawai'i."

"Well, I won't stand in the way of history," said Walt. He inked his signature purposefully above 'Dozer's famous logo and as an afterthought drew an arrow towards a rail and wrote, *This rail is nicer than the other one*"

Walt handed the marker to Kaleo. The Hawaiian took it but made no move to sign the board. He just stood next to it and laid a hand gently on the rail, staring down at the sun bleached wood with the aspect of a respectful pallbearer.

"It's okay, Kaleo, no shame. Go ahead and sign it," said 'Dozer, "Nothing fancy – just your name if you want."

Kaleo looked at him. 'Dozer could see the confusion on his face. He sighed and heaved himself to his feet and put his hand gently on Kaleo's shoulder. "Hey. …you don't have to sign the board if you don't feel like it."

Kaleo just stared vacantly at the board. He was remembering the day that 'Dozer had built it in his garage 45 years ago. The old gang had all been there, covered in wood dust and nagged by mosquitoes, watching Larson glue up the planks of balsa, a bottle of Primo in one hand and a pot of glue in the other. Kaleo could almost smell the dust and glue and resin. The tracing of resin drops had left a ghostly imprint of that very board on the cement of his garage floor. He had just looked at it this morning.

Finally he spoke. "Bruddah 'Dozer, I like sign your board. …but I cannot say how I feel about this board and us guys. I need sing one song. I cannot say 'em with words."

"Sure, Kaleo," said 'Dozer Larson gently, a lump in his throat. "Go ahead." He sat down quietly with the others. Sully handed him a beer and slung his arm over his shoulders.

Kaleo picked up his guitar and sat down alone on an empty tabletop. He took a few halting, shy strums on the guitar and, composing himself to his satisfaction, began to sing. It was an Hawaiian song, very old, sung in a quavering falsetto voice so porcelain delicate that it seemed impossible to attribute it to such a beefy and tough-looking individual.

The old friends listened to the beautiful and sad *mele* about homesickness. Warriors were on the march, far from home, high up in the cold and damp mountain passes. Sully and Clayton knew the Hawaiian words and followed the determined but lonesome warriors as they trudged through the mist, shivering in the cold, missing their families and homes. They sang of the world lost to them far, far below, now impossibly sweet and perhaps never to be seen again. The enemy waited, cloaked in fog, on the other side of the *pali*, their clubs and spears poised for the storm of combat that would decide who on that day would cross over into eternity.

'Dozer Larson knew scant few of the words but, as with so much of Hawaiian music, felt the homesickness coursing through the song. He found himself being flung forcibly back into the past – like the warriors in the *mele* he too longed for a time and place that was no more. One shard of time, utterly unbidden, pierced his mind. Now there was warm sunshine on his bare and tanned back. He was walking down the sand at Hale'iwa, his stomach tight as whipcord, trunks hanging loosely on his hips, the board under his arm sleek and lethal. The waves towered over the horizon, but he felt no fear, and turned to snap a mock salute to all the gang under the *lauhala* tree and they laughed and saluted him back and, damn, didn't it feel goddamned great to be young and at the top of your game with the sun burning on your shoulders.

Kaleo sang the refrain that says to the Hawaiian listener "let the story be told"; the last verse sent the warriors on towards an uncertain fate. Then the men dissolved into the mist and 'Dozer was hurled forty years into the present.

Kaleo laid the guitar down and went over and signed the board. 'Dozer sniffled. Joe 'Bulldozer' Larson had been a notorious hellraiser in his youth, plowing through huge surf and colossal bar fights with the same abandon, but the fiercest of men are often the most sentimental. Clayton, too, was glad he was wearing his tinted glasses. Sully saw this and nodded with satisfaction. The music and waterworks had already started and they weren't half out of beer yet.

"Goddammit, Kaleo, why did you have to go and do that," 'Dozer said, daubing a welling tear from one eye. "Now I've gotta go back inside looking like I've been blubbering."

"Ah, hell, Larson, just tell 'em you just went get our bar tab," joked Sully.

'Dozer hugged Kaleo, slapping his back with affection.

The quiet mood ended as the auditorium erupted in a riot of hooting and whistles.

"Geez, what is it now?" 'Dozer got up and went over to peek in the back door.

"Ho, these people sure do love those old boards," said Kimo.

Walt shot him a withering look. "What's going on in there is not about the *love* of surfboards."

'Dozer came back and sat down again. "It's the *wiliwili* board," he said, "Do you guys want to watch this one? Should be the highest bidding of the night."

"What *wiliwili* board?" asked Kimo.

"You didn't hear about that board?"

" The one that's supposed to be haunted?" asked Walt.

"Yeah, that's the one," replied 'Dozer, "Some guy on the mainland bought it at an estate sale. An old Hawaiian family had it, I guess. Took it back to California, but he freaked out after a while. Heard about this auction and called me up – begged me to sell it for him."

"He said it was haunted? You mean like one ghost board?" asked Kimo.

"Yup. Spooked the hell out of him. Ask Clayton. I referred the guy to him. That 'chicken skin' stuff is right up your alley, eh, Clayton."

"Chicken skin is right, bruddah 'Dozer," said Clayton. "That board never should have left Hawaii." He upended the last swig of a beer down his throat and sighed. "But it wasn't haunted mainland–kind like that. It was *auakua*, full of ghost bile."

Everyone moved to squeeze together at one table. Local people love a good ghost story; the Hawaiian is content to live side by side with the glimmer of departed ancestors and to respect deeply the workings of these spirits upon what the *haole* sees only as everyday objects. When a westerner writes of, say, "the living rock" he is being poetic. But when the

Hawaiian describes a stone as being "alive" he is saying that the *pohaku* does indeed have a soul.

"So, this *haole* guy went give me a call," continued Clayton, "and says he's got this surfboard, one *wiliwili* board, and that it's haunted and he cannot figure 'em out."

"How did he get it?" Walt asked.

"Like 'Dozer said, he bought it off of some estate sale. Local family. Had it listed on eBay, I guess. This *haole* guy, he's one big-time collector, so he just swooped right away. Flew over himself the next day and paid cash. I think the family was having hard time or something.

"Anyway, he takes the board back to California and hangs it on the wall in his living room. Some mansion-kind place in Mission Viejo - I think the guy's in real estate or something."

"Where's Mission Viejo?" interrupted Kimo.

"It's south, by San Clem-ofre something like that," said Sully. He'd been ushered up and down the coast for any number of tradeshows and surf contests. "Like Kapolei, except they get one Ralph's Supermarket and one In & Out Burger."

"In & Out Burger?"

"It's one drive in burger place, but they get all kind fresh stuffs," said Sully with growing enthusiasm, warming to the thought of food. "The bun is fresh, the lettuce is fresh and the meat stay one real patty. And the shakes are real ice cream, brah – ho, broke the mouth."

"Man, I'm getting hungry," said Kaleo, "How about we dig out and go up to that saimin stand on Beretania. One bowl with *char siu* and raw egg would be *un*-real."

"Brah, you've been out in the *kuahiwi*s too long," said Clayton, "That place is one Starbuck's now." He turned to regard the others. "So, you like hear the rest of the story, or what?"

"Shoots."

"Yeah."

"Sorry, bruddah."

"Okay." Clayton paused to marshal his thoughts. "Anyway, the guy hangs the board on the wall on these wooden racks but in the morning he comes down and sees the board laying on the floor. So he guesses it fell over during the night – figures it must have been an earthquake or something. No dings but, so he puts it back up in the racks. But every morning after that, same thing, the board stay laying on the floor."

"Ho, I'm getting chicken skin," said Kaleo.

"Tell 'em about the bee," said 'Dozer.

"Oh, yeah. There was one bumblebee in the board. The Hawaiians call them *meli la'au*, the carpenter bee, 'cause they always dig into the wood. You know how soft *wiliwili* wood is – easy for the bees to make *puka*s. This board had one bumblebee sealed in one of the *puka*s with amber or wax or something.

"So this guy is starting to freak out on this board, and one night it's real quiet and he can't sleep 'cause he's laying there just waiting to hear the clunk of the board falling down – but instead he thinks he can hear one sound like a baby crying"

"Ho! For real?" exclaimed Sully, holding out his arms to show the gooseflesh.

"Was the board on the ground the next morning?"

"Yeah," Clayton nodded. "It was on the ground."

"But why was the bee in the *puka*?"

"Well, after the guy described the board to me I called up my friend Butch down at the Bishop Museum. Wanted to see if he could find out something. Couple days later, he calls me up. Says that he knew exactly what board it was. Was easy because of the bee…

"Turns out that the board is over a hundred and fifty years old. One princess had it made for her infant daughter. The bumblebee in the *puka* was bright yellow, like gold – the queen bee. Maybe the princess hoped her baby girl would grow up and be queen too, one day."

Clayton paused and looked at Sully and Kaleo. "But she died of small pox at the age of three." It was a common fate that entwined all the branches of their family trees. "The princess came sick after that; by and by she died of one broken heart. The board was stored away somewhere," he shrugged. "It was never ridden...."

It was entirely dark now. The birds had gone silent in the banyan and the soft cool tradewinds rustled the coco palms high above them. Kaleo picked out a lush and moody tune in slack key that mirrored the rhythm of the fronds nodding overhead. They listened as the commotion inside crested again, envisioning the frantic runners, the crowd hooting as each bid was matched, the *wiliwili* board propped up in the harsh spotlights, and the auctioneer whose gavel would fall any second for the final time.

"So who's gonna get the board now," Walt wondered aloud for them all.

"Don't worry," said 'Dozer, "Butchie is in there with a blank check from the docents at the museum. And anybody that starts a bidding war with him is gonna have to deal with some pissed-off Hawaiians."

They all laughed. "Right on. So what happened with the board, Clayton? How did it get back here?"

"It was a funny thing, brah," said Clayton, "Every night this *haole* guy went put the board back on the wall and every morning it was back on the floor. Then, one day last month he went call me and said 'you know, every morning this board is lying on the floor, but it always points in the same direction. But today, for the first time, it was pointing the other way.'

"All of a sudden I went figure 'em out," Clayton went on, "It was weird. Remember last month we had those *kona* winds, first time in a long time? Before that it was trades for months, eh? Well, the day that we had that *kona* storm was the day that the *wiliwili* board went *huli* in one 'nother direction."

Clayton paused. As a child he had dreaded the late-night drives home after spending the day with his family on the rural leeward side. Today there are brightly lit suburbs and supermarkets there, but back then it had been a ten-mile stretch of narrow highway, black as a tunnel, that bored through the cane fields above the 'Ewa plain. His father would always say the same thing. "Look how dark it stay. Wouldn't want to break down here, would we, kids?" As Clayton cringed in the back seat his father would talk of the haunted ravines up there somewhere, "as a matter of fact, right above where we stay driving right now". There, he said, the *kupuna* warned of the forlorn and homeless ghosts that wandered amongst the *wiliwili* trees, and Clayton could still summon the childhood image of the lonely groves of trees that in pale moonlight looked like bony fingers poking out of agonized parched hide. The gentle northerly tradewinds made the trees wag slowly to and fro as if they were admonishing him to look away. The worst, he recalled, were the nights when the *kona* storm winds would lash in from the south and the *wiliwili* trees would flail restlessly under the attack, the tormented spirits adding their cries to the howling gale.

Clayton leaned forward and laid both his hands palms downward on the table. He noticed that they shook a little. "So I tell the guy. I went figure 'em out: it's the wind that keeps moving his board around. I told him that that *wiliwili* wood must have been cut out of one *kapu* grove somewhere."

"What did he say to that?" said Walt, spellbound.

"You know what he said?" replied Clayton, shaking his head, "He actually went say, 'I don't understand - how did the wind blow all the way over here into my living room?'"

Sully pounded the table and snorted. "Stupid *haole*. He think the wind went blow across the ocean," he laughed. "...But the wind went blow across *time.*"

Landfall

Willy Powers' life was on bald tires and no spare thought Lt. Pete Carnahan as he regarded the young lifeguard across the desk from him. He'd seen it many times before. Powers had gone from being one of his star guards to becoming an embarrassment to the Honolulu City and County Water Safety Division that Carnahan presided over.

They sat in Carnahan's office overlooking the shore at Ala Moana, Powers chewing his lip and brooding out the enormous tinted windows at the armada of surfers enjoying an early-summer swell. The lieutenant ignored the view, instead sipping his morning coffee and thumbing through the disciplinary report for the third time that day. The prospect of giving the young man his dressing-down held little appeal to Carnahan and he was doubly irritated that Powers had been late, keeping him from his morning training swim.

Willy Powers had been blowing it all summer. Carnahan flipped through the file again and made up his mind. He slid the document towards the center of the desk. Everything he needed to know was written on the errant lifeguard's face. The eyes were puffy, bloodshot, and he had lost his suntan. Then there was the shaved head, the raw, still–weeping tattoo on one bicep. Probably a result, observed Carnahan, of the drinking and partying connected with another boring, wave–less summer on the North Shore. It was the same old story. The young man had just turned thirty in June and no one, least of all Willy Powers himself, could be sure whether he had been celebrating or mourning.

The previous week he'd been driving a City and County truck and had gotten himself into an impromptu drag race with one of his rivals, a big–wave surfer also mired in the summer doldrums. Powers forgot to strap down the rescue surfboard and it flew off the racks, striking a rental car. The Japanese tourist at the wheel veered into a tree but fortunately was unhurt.

Carnahan drummed on the desk and leveled as stern a gaze as he could muster upon Powers.

"Look, Willy, I've recommended to the disciplinary board that you be suspended without pay for three weeks. It's the best I can do, seeing as how this last incident made the papers."

"Thanks, sir..." said Willy, relieved. The boom hadn't crashed down as hard as he'd expected.

"But..." continued Carnahan, ".... The other things that haven't made the papers – well, next time I'll wash you right out of Water Safety. You'll consider yourself damned lucky to get a position guarding a baby pool at the YMCA."

Powers' head drooped.

Carnahan couldn't be sure whether he was ashamed or hung over. Probably both. The kid wasn't a bad sort, he thought – he just thrived on action. Surfers made the best lifeguards where high surf was concerned but they were an independent and undisciplined bunch. Many of these types went stale in the summer months. Willy Powers was of that breed which can weather any storm but whose nervous system shatters in a calm.

Carnahan, like most every surfer and lifeguard on Oahu, had a certain grudging respect for Powers' abilities in extreme conditions. Nearly every surfer on the North Shore would like to make a name for himself – those who pretended otherwise even more so. If they didn't want to, reasoned Carnahan, why were they there at all?

Willy Powers had made a name for himself, but lately he had been taking awful chances to keep that name on the marquee. During the previous winter's largest swell he had paddled out from Shark's Cove, a cruel, serrated battlement of lava rock behind Waimea Bay. A twenty-foot swell was running, and if he had mistimed his jump from the rocks would have been hammered into pulp on the jagged reef. Still, Powers hadn't come out of the venture unscathed, as he proceeded to paddle straight into the middle of a big-wave tournament taking place at Waimea and, after refusing to leave the line-up, received two black eyes in the ensuing scuffle with the water patrol.

These kids were all like that nowadays, mused Carnahan. More talent than the previous generation but with none of the discipline. This modern youth truly puzzled him; they seemed an incurious, disaffected lot who, seeing nothing left to create or explore, either set out to deface or destroy themselves – or gape from the sidelines at others doing so.

Then again, perhaps Powers just needed something to focus on. He had the faint glimmering of an idea:

"You're out of shape, Willy," he said, taking another tack, "and you know Water Safety won't tolerate that. You probably wouldn't pass the swim test right now. ...Not to mention a drug test."

The young lifeguard offered no word in his defense. He just sat there with slumped shoulders. Carnahan unbent a little.

"Look, I want you to consider something. You know about the Molokai paddleboard race? Well, it's six weeks away. I want you to enter."

Powers started out of his reverie and gaped at him.

"What? C'mon, skipper, there's not enough time to train for that race. You're talkin' about 32 miles! It would take, like, at least six months to get ready for that."

"So what?" Carnahan snapped. "Then go 'tourist class'. There's a team event, too. A relay deal. Hook up with Grant -- he wants to do it and needs a partner. Six weeks is plenty of time to get in shape. Half of that time you'll be suspended from work anyway."

"I don't know, sir," said Powers, "just paddling? I mean, that's kinda boring."

Since the jet skis had become the primary Water Safety rescue tool many of the younger guards had completely forsaken the old rescue paddleboards.

"I'd rather spend the time off over in Kailua. I've been doin' some kiteboardin' in the off-season, you know, so I can keep on it for the tow-ins next winter..."

Carnahan shook his head. At fifty-one years old was more than a little old fashioned, and held these newfangled 'extreme sports' in disdain. He had come into lifeguarding not from the surfing set but the Coast Guard and tried to shape his command to conform to a decidedly military pattern. Carnahan lumped any and all non-functional derring-do into a category disdainfully reserved for daredevils and flagpole sitters, and regarded much of what his surfing employees did, though admittedly exciting, as unduly frivolous.

"No. It's either the race or the city rehab program. You'd rather drive into town for classes everyday for six months?"

He paused.

"Look, I know all you guys want to be cowboys on the skis, but paddleboards are what lifesaving is all about. Every great guard has done distance paddling."

Powers sulked, fidgeting with a scale model of the Hawaiian sailing canoe *Hokule'a* Carnahan kept on his desk.

"Besides, Willy," he continued, nodding at the model, "you need to learn the difference between an inshore waterman and an open ocean waterman."

"Alright, already, skipper," sighed Powers, beaten. "I guess it seems like the thing to do, huh?"

*　　　　　*　　　　　*

The Molokai Challenge is regarded as the toughest paddleboard race in the world. The channel that lies between the west end of Molokai and the eastern shores of Oahu is one of the roughest in the tropics, torn by frequent gales and besieged with massive currents. In a field of a hundred paddlers there will be a hundred stories, every one of them recounted stroke by stroke as each exhausted racer stumbles ashore on Oahu. No one has an easy time of it. Some will kiss the sand upon arriving and vow to stick to shorter races, and others never gain the finish line at all.

On the morning of the race Powers and his partner Grant rose before dawn to eat their breakfast well ahead of the start time. They had trained hard over the preceding six weeks, and Powers had come to feel that he had a tough and reliable partner in the lanky young guard who worked the Sandy Beach tower. Since they were to paddle in a relay system, most of their training had been comprised of shorter, tougher sprints mixed with a 10-mile practice race against the wind once a week. If every thing went well, they reasoned, each should only have to paddle about eight segments of twenty-five minutes apiece.

They finished their bananas and toast and washed it all down with scalding black coffee. Gear was checked and re-checked and the two took turns basting one another with sunscreen. Powers affixed the decal with their race number on it to the nose of their paddleboard.

Then there was nothing left to do but head down to the shoreline and join the growing armada of paddlers and their escort boats jockeying for room in the small bay from which the race would soon commence.

Everyone was busy. First-timers paced about, anxiously nibbling on energy bars, while the veteran paddlers sat off to one side and calmly stretched or tried to relax their breathing.

As the sun rose over the palm trees the paddlers were called together for the Hawaiian *pule*, or prayer, and everyone gathered in a circle around the white-frocked *kahu* with bowed heads. First there was a chant, and then a prayer, both in Hawaiian. Powers noticed that one of the local paddlers had tears streaming down his face. He was puzzled, but as he had been raised in the islands it soon dawned on him that while he was about to paddle across the Molokai channel for a T-shirt and a trophy this young Hawaiian paddler was evidently in communion with his ancestors. No doubt the same benediction had been bestowed upon countless generations of Polynesians preparing to push their canoes from the shore with their very lives staked upon their seamanship.

The paddlers lined up at the mouth of the bay, holding hands to keep in formation as the northeast tradewinds awoke and began to flick whitecaps seaward into the channel yawning before them. The horn sounded and the whole line flung forward, ninety pairs of arms churning as each paddler tried desperately to claw ahead of the others and away from the turbulence created by the tangle of flailing arms.

Watching from the escort boat, Willy Powers noticed a few of the contestants already pulling away from the main pack. Grant had agreed to paddle the first leg and Powers soon spotted him in the middle of the group, scrambling all out to break away up to the windward edge of the crowd. The course from Molokai to Oahu draws a fairly straight east-to-west line, but the tradewinds slant across the channel a little from the north of east. The veteran paddler tries to surf the wind-driven waves as much as possible – yet must be careful not to be lured into the trap of following this free ride on the "conveyor belt" too far to the south and thus face slogging uphill to the north later in the day, when he is exhausted, against the wind and current to reach the finish line near Koko Head. Thus the experienced paddler hoards his position to windward like a miser, waiting until the latter half of the race to spend it in a final 'downhill' run home.

Twenty minutes into the race the pack was spread out over a quarter mile or so. Powers directed the captain of their escort boat to a place about fifty feet in front of Grant and dove into the water. As Grant came abreast he rolled off the board and Powers swung himself onto the deck in one fluid motion. A line was thrown to Grant, the boat throttled back, and he pulled himself over the transom. This would be the routine for the rest of the race.

Already the seas were curling and foaming at the top. It was going to be a windy day. Powers thrilled at the rush of speed as he surfed down each wave, and set about trying to link crest to crest into one unbroken chain of downhill slides. They had chosen a stock–class 12' paddleboard, believing that it would fit into the tight and steep wind waves better than a longer board. The board glided forward with the slightest effort and, optimistic about their chances of getting across in less than six hours, Powers tested the torque in his shoulders and arms, pushing up the rpms until he could feel heat seeping from the muscles. He felt good and strong.

Then, things began to go wrong.

Trouble began when he realized the chin rest hadn't been properly shaped: as water rushed over the deck the little wedge of foam directed a sheet of spray right into his face. He pulled his goggles down from his forehead – and they instantly fogged up. The reduction in visibility caused him to mistime waves; he felt suddenly nauseous so he pulled them off again.

They were now three miles out and the pack split into two distinct groups, one heading north and the other lured south by the run of the seas.

The wind grew steadily and began to whistle through the rigging of the boat. A squall hovered overhead. The water turned black and rain pelted them with fat drops that stung like birdshot. Powers climbed back aboard after his first turn and heard on the CB radio that the leaders were a half-mile ahead, a little north and west of them. Now that he had stopped paddling it was cold. He wrapped himself in a towel and sipped some Gatorade.

The boat pitched wildly on all axes and Powers had to brace himself as he sat on one of the huge coolers that were secured along the gunwales. Shivering, he felt his first misgivings about the crossing, noticing that Oahu was still a featureless smear on the horizon and that Molokai remained very close astern.

At five miles out they lost their chin rest. It was Powers' turn paddling; he caught the nose while pitching down a steep wind wave. The board started to broach and before he could pull out of it Powers was flipped over into a roll. The chin rest was gone when he climbed back onto the paddleboard. A small thing, yet it was an enormous setback. Now they had to support the full weight of their heads for the rest of the race.

Soon Powers had a splitting headache. He had never in all his life been seasick, and was genuinely shocked with the realization that he was about to be. After climbing aboard the escort boat following his turn he suddenly felt weak and nauseated. His head, from the base of the neck up to his temples, throbbed as if it was being squeezed in a vise. The boat wallowed ahead in idle, pitching and rolling as if on carnival gimbals. The diesel exhaust made his stomach churn in rebellion and a stale, ashtray taste in his mouth made him want to retch. Afraid of dehydration, he didn't dare throw up. The few sips of Gatorade he managed to swallow tasted like antifreeze.

All Willy Powers could do was slump down onto the cooler and miserably await his next turn.

Thus the pattern for the rest of the day was set. When Powers was paddling the effort of holding his head up gave him an unbearable headache and he couldn't wait to crawl back onto the boat. Once aboard, the excruciating nausea he suffered made him long for his turn back on the paddleboard. Grant and the rest of the crew seemed utterly unaffected. They were seasoned fishermen and maddeningly immune to the agonies he endured. Watching them eat their thick greasy sardine sandwiches bursting with mayonnaise made his stomach heave in disgust. So Powers sat in a limbo of fatigue, wretched and alone in his misery, alternately pleading with and cursing the stopwatch that would enable him to trade one form of suffering for another.

Sometime later they ran into a belt of wind–blown man–o–war jellyfish. Powers was stung badly by one that washed over his legs. It burned as if a red–hot coal has been dropped onto his flesh but he could not stop paddling and risk broaching again. A fresh and stronger wave of nausea swept through him. It took tremendous effort to keep from vomiting even as he paddled. Still, he tried to hold to his pace, not wanting to let Grant down nor surrender their tenuous position in the middle of the pack.

Midway across the channel Powers began to admit to himself that they would never make it. This was the open ocean now. With nothing to impede it, the wind pressed its full force upon the pitching, toppling seas. It was chaotic, deafening, unreadable. Powers remembered what Lt. Carnahan had said to him that day in his office, that there was a big difference between an inshore waterman and an open-ocean waterman. He saw the truth in that now.

A huge, angry squall line banked up against Oahu, completely obscuring the island. They were forced to paddle their course by compass. He dared not look back and be unmanned by the sight of Molokai still so close behind. This was a 'death march' now and Powers forced himself to think of other things, taking shelter in that mental storm cellar that all people who find themselves in tests of endurance must eventually turn to.

He grew so weak that he was barely able to climb up the transom of the escort boat at the end of each turn on the paddleboard. The sun beat cruelly down upon him but he was far too exhausted to go into the cabin and rummage through his duffel for the sunscreen. For a while he tried to nibble on a candy bar but couldn't gather enough saliva to swallow the tiniest morsel. After a while he realized the cooler he rested on was full of fish. The ice was melting in the heat and the stench assailed him, yet he hadn't the strength to move elsewhere. Powers had always believed that seasickness was all about vomiting and was blindsided by the fatigue. He thought he'd never been so tired in all his life. Wrapped in his towel he tried to nap while perched on the cooler but the boat violently lurched each time he succeeded in nodding off. He could only wobble there on his seat wearily watching Grant take stroke after stroke, glancing at the stopwatch with a strange mixture of anticipation and dread. Eight more minutes, now five, get ready to jump in... now two more minutes...

In every race there is a turning point. This time it came ten miles off Oahu. Powers had just crawled aboard after another tough slog and heard the radio say the leading paddlers were battling a strong head current near the area where the ocean floor began to shelve sharply up towards the island. Many of the contestants had gone too far north and were unable to make any headway against the current.

Soon a number of contestants had given up and dropped out of the race. One of the top-ranked paddlers cramped up like a seized engine and had to be hauled aboard in a sling. Another boat radioed that it had suffered trouble with a propeller shaft. By the strict rules laid down by the race organizers the paddler could not continue on his own. Powers heart leapt at the news – he was sorely tempted to throw in the towel as well and wanted ample company in the shame.

The last eight miles was the worst. Powers and Grant paddled mechanically, turn after turn, yet the island stubbornly refused to draw closer. Grant was red-faced but still intent. Powers, to whom time and distance were warped by seasickness and fatigue, felt that he could barely remember not being teased by the craters and mountains of East Oahu beckoning behind the sea spray, seemingly so close, yet unreachable.

It was in this Limbo period that Powers faced his breaking point. For hours, it seemed, the coastline refused to draw nearer. The head current was so strong he felt as if he was paddling in place on an enormous treadmill, yet he couldn't relax his mind for a moment – one lapse in concentration and a paddler would find himself overtaken and broached by the towering seas that ceaselessly herded him forward. Aboard the boat the radio crackled again and again; more contestants were dropping out – the fierce current taking its toll. The temptation to quit grew irresistible. Powers thought how easy it would be to crawl back aboard the boat and say the few simple words that would see them blasting away at full throttle from the pitiless, heaving nightmare. Yet he couldn't let his partner down – and the grim prospect of failure, of facing Lt. Carnahan ashore. Tears of frustration welled up in his bloodshot eyes. But he paddled on.

Pain began to sear up his left arm from elbow to shoulder. He was losing torque in that arm now. It became more and more difficult to catch the waves. Soon he began to hear the splash of his tiring arms as they plopped erratically into the water – the death rattle of the long-distance paddler. Grant yelled encouragement from the boat but to Powers it seemed to echo feebly down a dark windy tunnel toward him. Disconnect the mind from the body, he thought, become a machine. A machine feels nothing, creates only heat and energy. He daydreamed of his bed back at the hotel on Molokai, no doubt lying there still unmade, warm and tantalizing. Each arm was raised and plunked into the water, over and over again – another two hundred, three hundred strokes and then he could be hauled up into the boat.

Finally the shoreline grew perceptibly closer. With five miles to go they began to recognize landmarks around Sandy Beach and Hanauma Bay. Other paddlers began merging into a single pack again as they churned into the final leg along Koko Head. When Powers came abreast the growing mass of paddlers he was genuinely shocked to realize he and Grant would make it after all. The sudden surge of strength from the pride of being amongst the others genuinely shocked him. No longer competitors but comrades, he saw in each of their haggard and lined faces the same trials he had endured. As they gained Koko Head the current slackened and the little group whooped out a ragged cheer, joined by the bleats of horns and sirens from the escort boats. Powers and Grant hooted until their throats were raw.

After thirty miles of open ocean a landfall was ahead. The channel, if not conquered, would be survived.

Powers relieved Grant as they reached the shelter of the sea cliffs beneath Koko Head. The ocean was calmer now and the seasickness vanished. A fair current sluiced along the base of the cliffs and he edged into it to sprint the last few miles around the headland and towards the finish at the mouth of Maunalua Bay.

He crossed the finish line fifteen minutes later, wobbling unsteadily ashore as the gathered crowd greeted each finisher with a *lei* and genuine applause.

It had been seven-and-a-half hours since the crack of the starting gun, a rather undistinguished time that put Powers and Grant somewhere in the middle of the field. And yet...even the top guys looked utterly worn out.

All readily agreed that the conditions had been particularly brutal this year and one third of the starters hadn't made it ashore at all.

*   *   *

"That's the hardest trip in the world, man," boasted Powers. "Fifth place in our age division! And everyone is saying we had the worst conditions ever."

The awards ceremony was over. Grant and his grandfather, Bob, who had come to pick them up with his grandson's truck, stood listening to Powers' account of the race. Willy was working on his third Corona and it had gone to his head on account of his empty stomach and sunburn.

"Yeah, it was tough," he swaggered, "but we made it. Huh, Grant? Showed 'em, didn't we?"

"Yeah, Willy, we made it all right," agreed Grant, thinking about all the paddlers that had done it solo and finished hours ahead of them – – and of how Powers, game as he was, had crapped out on him in the middle of the channel, adding at least an hour to their time.

He shrugged. "Hey, I'm going to go and pull the truck around so we can load up"

Grant left, walking away unsteadily as he tried to regain his shore legs.

The grandfather turned to Powers. He was a tall elderly man with a shock of white hair set in contrast to a ruddy and lined face.

"Well, that's just super, you guys," he beamed. "I'm glad Grant found a partner. He really had his heart set on doing this race."

Powers waved a deprecating hand. "Next year we'll train harder…" Now he was the veteran airily dismissing a shabby effort to an admiring fan. "… Get a seventeen-footer, maybe. Shave an hour off our time, easy."

"Oh, sure, sure," agreed Bob. "You guys will do better next year."

He fished out a cigar from his shirt pocket and lit it. He squinted at Powers. "Grant said you were a little seasick. Must have been kinda' tough out there."

"Oh, man, you've got no idea how rough it can be out there," Powers said. In a lower voice he admitted, "I'll tell you, I was pretty, well, choked up when we made our landfall"

A strange expression flickered across Bob's face, a flinch that morphed almost instantly into a somewhat pained grin. Powers, alarmed, thought the old man might be having chest pains.

"Yep, landfalls can be pretty emotional," agreed the elderly man, his blue eyes piercing through a wreath of cigar smoke. "I remember coming across the channel and...."

"You paddled the channel?" interrupted Powers, puzzled. "I didn't know. ...Did they have this race way back then?"

"The English Channel, son."

Powers looked at him blankly. "I don't understand – what race...?"

"I was a waist gunner on a B–17. Stationed in England," said the grandfather, releasing another deep draught of cigar smoke. "This was back in '43, of course."

"But. ...Wait a minute," Powers stammered, "Weren't you. ...I mean, aren't you too young to have been in the war?"

"Well, I'm 76." he replied. "I went in when I was 16, you know, after Pearl Harbor. Faked my age. Like a lot of guys. I'd rolled my Ford and lost my sweetheart to some joker in uniform – all in the same week – so I figured, 'what the hell'. Seemed like the thing to do."

Powers fumbled, at a loss. He had only the vaguest ideas about history, formed mostly by an osmotic intake from television.

"Cool. ...What was it like?" he asked – it was the only thing he could think of to say.

The older man peered at him from across the canyon of sixty years and nodded towards the channel.

"Well, it was kinda' like what you guys did today."

He smiled. This was impossible. He hadn't talked about it in years.

"We were cold, tired and sick. Scared shitless a lot of the time. The B-17 aircraft was a bomber, you know. Every mission was over enemy territory. German fighter planes gave us hell, but the flak was worse. It would come through the fuselage, white hot, with hardly a sound - kinda' like a screwdriver punching a hole in a can. That's how I got this."

He pointed to a puckered mass of scar tissue along his jaw line.

"Bit of flak got me in the jaw here - but I couldn't feel sorry for myself at the time, since our bombardier was sitting right there across from me with his leg blown off."

He paused, swallowing hard.

"Bled to death right in front of me, the poor sonuvabitch."

There was a momentary glimpse of the Inferno reflected in his eyes. Then he stitched a wan smile on his face and it was gone. Over the years he'd gotten pretty good at slamming the furnace door shut.

For a thoughtful minute he puffed on his cigar. The kid hadn't squirmed away, so he went on.

"Yep, more than anything I just remember being cold and tired. In fact, that's the thing I remember the most. It was so darned cold up there - as soon as you poured the coffee out of the Thermos it was ice-cold already. And the fatigue - just drop-dead tired, nothing like it."

Was the kid listening? He was a lifeguard; that was something, at least.

"There's a kind of exhaustion where you just don't care anymore, where you'd even welcome death as a chance to sleep. Hell, even the pilots would nod off sometimes. ...One time..."

He stopped, looking sidelong at the young man. How long had he been blathering on?

"Anyway, don't want to bore you with a bunch of old war stories. It was all a long, long time ago..."

Powers felt all the exhaustion of the day returning. He absently sipped the last of his beer. It was warm and tasted bitter. He shifted his weight to his other leg. The earlier sense of redemption was gone, clouded over.

"No, no, it's cool..." he trailed off.

"Anyway, I know what you mean about landfalls," the old man said, trying to get back onto common ground.

"Coming back from a mission the crew would be listening on our radio sets about all the trouble the other fellows in the formation were getting in. Some were all shot up and had to crash–land into enemy territory, others had to ditch into the Channel. Sometimes, well, they never had a chance.

"One mission we'd been torn up pretty bad by a bunch of 109s that charged us head-on over Antwerp. We lost an engine, and once that happened you couldn't keep up and had to fall out of the formation, so you'd be a sitting duck for fighters. Luckily the weather had turned snotty and we dove into some clouds here and there and were able to dodge our way towards the Channel."

The old man stabbed his cigar in the air, tapping out little puffs of smoke about him.

"Then, pock – pock – pock! Flak batteries on the coast got us – lost another engine and shredded half a stabilizer."

"Well now, we limped across the Channel on the last two engines, flying under the clouds 'cause we simply didn't have enough power to claw our way above them. Had our chutes on, ready to bail. Pilot's legs were shaking from the strain of holding out against the rudder pedals. Finally. ... We could see the coast of England ahead and it was as if all the tension just –

whoosh – left your body. I felt absolutely drained, almost too tired to think – then suddenly beneath us there was green instead of gray. Good old England. You know, hedgerows, little cottages with smoke curling up from the chimneys. ...Had to be the most wonderful sight I've ever seen."

Grant was making his way back to them now, accompanied by the newly arrived Lt. Carnahan. The Lieutenant greeted Powers warmly and was introduced to Grant's grandfather.

"All right, Water Safety! Way to go, fellas," said Carnahan, shaking their hands. "How was it out there?"

Powers seemed curiously deflated. Carnahan had expected him to be strutting in full plumage.

The young lifeguard only pawed sheepishly at the grass with his bare toes.

"It was okay," he drawled, "We made it across."

Carnahan squinted at him, puzzled.

"Hmmm. Well, I'm on my way to a meeting. Just wanted to congratulate you both. I'll see you guys at headquarters tomorrow."

He gave Powers a final searching glance and, satisfied, turned away and left them.

The shadows were lengthening and the crowd had gone. A work crew was taking down the tents and gathering up rubbish while mynah birds noisily haggled over the abandoned trays of food.

Powers felt flushed. The sunburn was catching up with him and his bare scalp was tender and pink. He turned his bloodshot eyes towards Grant's grandfather. The shrapnel scar was a livid welt on the old man's chin. It would have been fun, back in the tower the next day, telling the other guys how 'insane' it had been. But now...

"Hey, Grant," said Powers, "You never told me your grandfather was such...such a hell-man."

"Oh, yeah," replied Grant, "The war stuff, you mean? Was he busting out some of his stories?"

Grant turned to his grandfather.

"How many was it, again, grandpa?" he asked, "How many missions did you fly?"

The old man shrugged.

"Oh, sixty-two or sixty-three sorties, I forget. ...Anyway..." He ground out his cigar and flung it away. He slapped his grandson affectionately on the back. "All ready to go, fellas?" he asked. And then, without a trace of irony, added, "I'll drive - you guys must be beat."

Bluebirds At Midnight

On a moonlit summer night in Honolulu a young Hawaiian man named Makali'i decided to turn off the television and go night surfing. Makali`i – named after the stars of the summer sky – slid his father's old Surfline Hawaii longboard into the back of the truck and bounced down the road that sloped from the ancient volcano upon which crouched the little community of Hawaiian and local–born people. Ten minutes later he stood in Waikiki, surfboard in arm, gaped at by strangers as he waited to cross Kalakaua Avenue.

The stoplight changed and Makali`i crossed, relieved to be free of the cement. Not until he gained the other side did he allow himself to feel any excitement about the waves he would ride. He often surfed at night. He hated the Town surf crowds and avoided all widely broadcast swells, day or night. On a full moon like tonight the crowds were just as bad as at midday. But a new southwest swell was arriving and he hoped it would be big enough to break on the outer reefs, far from the reach of the full moon surfing cult that clogged the inshore breaks.

Makali`i strode past the Duke Kahanamoku statue, dodging the tourists that stopped in his path to goggle at the bronze figure looming over them. Head down, taking care to avoid eye contact, Makali`i saw enough out of the corner of his eye to tick off from his checklist all the various species of the Waikiki after-dark menagerie. There were the sullen and pasty hookers, tightly woven schools of Japanese, sun-broiled Canadians, and of course the ubiquitous crank with a parrot squatting on his shoulder. All turned to stare at Makali`i as he passed. Once again, the familiar resentment stung him, an Hawaiian feeling out of place in his own land because he was brown and shirtless and carrying a surfboard a stone's throw from the birthplace of surfriding.

Cautiously lifting his eyes, he saw a fat red-faced *haole* man clamber up onto the pedestal that supported the statue of Duke. His soft breasts jiggled beneath his gaudy floral print shirt as he draped a *lei* over one of Duke's arms; then his wife handed him a shiny, multi-colored surfboard. He held it beside him and flashed a shaka sign as she raised her camera and snapped a picture. Makali`i noticed with grim satisfaction that the surfboard was finless and had no coat of wax. The price tag was probably still stuck on it.

Makali`i stood in the shadows at the edge of the crowd for a moment and beheld the statue. The metal Duke, his arms thrown wide in what the sculptor no doubt felt was a gesture of '*aloha*,' glinted with each camera flash. "*Aloha* also means 'good-bye,'" thought Makali`i savagely. Or was that his father talking, he wondered. Just now it seemed that Duke's outstretched arms weren't welcoming visitors, but raised to halt something, beseeching some malignant force to stop. Why was he facing Town instead of the blue sea he loved, doomed for all time to confront the steel-spined tumors that choked off the tradewinds. The very tradewinds that once fanned the scent of plumeria down to the warm yellow sands – yup, that was his Pop talking, Makali'i decided. Pop grumbled about a lot of things, but he hadn't been down to Waikiki since Mom died and he came to take apart her lei stand and pack it away.

"Duke never even belong to us anymore," Pop once said. Some coast *haoles* had bought the rights to his name. Now there remained only lawsuits and counter suits, a pile of unfashionable garments with Duke's name embroidered on them, and a statue with its back turned to the sea. "Oh, and then of course there's old Kao," Pop continued, "telling the same old *bu lai* story how he went beat Duke in one canoe race. And where's Duke to set 'em straight? I tell you boy, plenty people like put words in his mouth."

Makali`i continued on, flitting through the

crowd, expertly swinging and dipping his surfboard to avoid striking the shuffling tourists. Finally he stepped onto the beach and all the tension in him slackened as his toes dug into the cool nighttime sand. Away from the glare of the street he searched the velvet black sea for signs of surf. As his eyes adjusted he saw that each break offshore Waikiki twinkled with smears of pearly white foam. A pretty good swell, he thought, allowing himself a tiny hope that the outside reefs would be breaking. He wanted to surf alone.

Wading into the blood–warm seawater, Makali`i set the board on the surface and pushed it out alongside him until the water was deep enough. Then he deftly sprang into a kneeling position on its deck. He let the current pull him out along the breakwall at Baby Queen's, paddling slowly until he cleared the outcrops of reef. Pop would be angry if he broke off the skeg.

Approaching the line–up at Queen's, he

was disappointed to discover a swarm of surfers already there. Even approaching midnight it was packed. Crestfallen, Makali'i sat for a moment in the channel between Queen's and Canoe's and watched the confused tangle of regulars and tourists as they scrambled and bleated and flailed into the waves. Most of the locals wore glow bands so they wouldn't be run over by *malihini*, or newcomers. To Makali'i the scene resembled a carnival at night – the glow bands whirling around in Ferris wheel circles and whipping into firefly swaths of neon roller coasters.

Makali'i was just about to settle for the weak and formless rollers of Canoe's when, far outside of Queen's Surf, he noticed a brushstroke of whitewater. Cunha's was breaking! Without a second thought he began paddling out toward the flash of soup. It would be difficult to line up out there, so far from the glare of the hotel lights, but he always loved the thrill of gliding down the thick–sloped waves of

Cunha's.

The farther he paddled the darker it got. Little by little the noise of the city diminished. The water grew colder and he knew he was halfway there, over the deep drop-off that separated Queen's from Cunha's. He felt calmer already. Each outer break gained was another rung climbed into the attic of the past. If he paddled out far enough, thought Makali'i, he could almost forget the karaoke bars and the throbbing boom boxes and the throngs of tourists waddling through their Internet Bargain Holidays.

Now on his wet skin he felt the cool tradewinds as they knitted back together after being baffled by the palisade of high rises. Then the seaward horizon seemed to tilt and blacken and there came from the darkness a sound like bats' wings rustling in flight. It was an approaching swell, hard to see because Cunha's was a fringing type of wave and whitewater rarely spilled down the entire face.

Makali'i hurried to reach the spot where he estimated the wave had first reared up - better to zero in on the line-up quickly to be ready for the next set. As the black wave glided toward him he was astonished to see a white slash sizzling down its face. Someone was already surfing Cunha's! Then there was a splash and the track vanished. The fat swell oiled toward Makali'i, blotting out the lower-hung stars in the sky. He was just about to call out when a dark snout smashed into the rail of his surfboard. Startled, he flung out his arms to ward off what he assumed was an attacking shark, but his hands found only the familiar form of a rider-less surfboard. He sat, heart pumping, and held the wayward board next to him. It was a strange board, almost as long as a canoe, with thick, square rails and a blunt nose. Curious, he rapped the deck with his knuckles. It sounded hollow and made of wood.

Makali'i draped a leg over the nose of the huge surfboard and began towing it seaward.

"Hey! *Hui*! *Hui*!" he called out, his eyes straining to discover the lost rider in the blackness.

Then, from out of the murk came first a shapeless cavity in the dark which became a shape and then a man, breast–stroking toward him with the precise, snappy stroke of a well–trained athlete obviously at ease swimming in the dark a half–mile out to sea.

"Here you go," said Makali'i as the swimmer neared him. He pushed the board in the direction of the man.

The man raised a hand in greeting and thanks, and then swung spryly up onto the enormous surfboard as if it were a horse.

"Thanks, son," said the man in a strong yet quiet voice. "Thought she was gonna wash up the Ala Wai."

Makali'i regarded his new companion. He was an elderly *haole* man with a trim build. His arms and shoulders were lean and sinewy like the roots of a banyan tree. His white hair ringed his balding pate in a thick crescent, glowing in the moonlight as if phosphorescent.

"No worries, Uncle," replied Makali'i. "How's the waves out here?"

"Oh, they're coming nice." The man turned to regard him for the first time. The eyes beneath the white eyebrows were those of an owl and Makali'i suddenly felt the breeze playing acutely on his spine.

"Mind if I join you, Uncle?" asked Makali'i. He had been raised in the island way and respected his elders, even if they were strangers.

"Sure, sure, boy," said the old man. "C'mon, it's really starting to build now."

The strange old man turned his giant board out to sea and began to paddle back out. Makali'i followed shyly a board length behind, watching the man propel his old wooden board with a classic butterfly stroke. After they had paddled two hundred yards or so the elder surfer abruptly stopped and sat up and took his bearing with swift bird-like pivots of his head.

Satisfied, he beckoned Makali'i to come sit by him.

They sat in the dark, rising and falling with the heaving inky swells that were marching up from the frozen nether-seas of the planet, begat by storm winds so cold they hurt a man's teeth to bare them to its winds. In the eerie silence, Makali'i had an odd feeling that he was adrift in a strange current ... pulling him - not to another time or place but into some strange wrinkle in consciousness. To reassure himself he turned and looked back to find some emotional anchorage in the glittering, twinkling lights of Town. He felt he should say something to break the spell.

"I don't know anyone who surfs without a leash anymore," he said. "Especially way out here in the middle of the night."

"I love to swim," was the old man's simple reply.

Makali'i could see that he certainly had a swimmer's body, though slim and wiry from asceticism as much as exercise. He wore his short swim trunks up over his navel in the old style.

"Sometimes goin' after your board is as much of an adventure as riding the dang thing," added the old man.

"Still, not many surfers swim at all anymore," said Makali'i.

"Well," said the old man, thoughtful, "when I first came here it was all one and the same thing with the Hawaiians I knew. Swimming, surfriding, paddling – all the same thing. In fact, it was because I was a swimmer that I came here in the first place."

"When was that, Uncle?"

"Oh, let me see … sometime in the early `20s, I guess. It was because of Duke Kahanamoku, you see…"

"You knew Duke?" blurted Makali'i.

"Oh, no. …Not at first, anyway. Later I did, but I first met him at a theater in Detroit – they were showing a newsreel of Duke swimming in the `20 Olympics. Well, I'd never seen anything like it. Hung around in the lobby after the movie and made sure I shook his hand."

The old man smiled as he remembered.

"Took it as my own engraved invitation to Hawai'i," he laughed. "But, of course everyone felt that way with Duke."

Makali'i felt a surging chill of 'chicken skin' creep up his spine and tickle the hair on the back of his neck. Duke had died an elderly man when Makali'i was a small child. He said nothing, his mind fumbling with the arithmetic of years.

"I still remember that handshake," went on the old man. "Duke had huge hands and even bigger feet. The beach boys used to joke that he could steer a canoe by dragging those big *luau* feet of his in the water..."

They sat in unearthly silence for a while, two lone surfers a half–mile off the Waikiki shoreline. Diamond Head glowed in the moonlight like a black–light sphinx, framing the old man with a vaporous halo as he sat staring out to sea, lost in thought, apparently picking at the elastic fabric of time.

A number of *malolo*, or flying fish, broke the surface and skittered over the water with a sound like a riffled deck of cards. Makali'i's heart leapt. He had loved them since he was a boy.

"Pop says they fly farther at night," he said.

"Their wings don't dry out so quick in the dark, I reckon," observed the old man.

Finally a set came, each cresting wave rustling like the wings of night birds. The elder surfer turned and was gone – Makali'i could hear his joyous cackle as he slid shoreward. Then a heaving black hill was lifting him up; Makali'i snapped around, took two strokes, climbed to his feet and instantly went sizzling down the face of the thick steep wave. The gliding sensation he felt at Cunha's always reminded him of the remembered thrill of his first wave at Baby Queen's when he was four. And the dark –

like a blindfold – only enhanced the sense of speed.

The old man was waiting where his wave had shrugged him off in the deeper water. Makali'i coasted to a stop near him. Invigorated, they turned to paddle back out, both laughing in sheer delight.

"It's getting bigger," crowed the old man. "When the tide's lower it might start breaking *outside*."

He pointed out to the inky void of the open ocean.

"Castle's?" asked Makali'i, puzzled. The shortboard era had long ago drawn all the surfers into the shorebreaks, leaving that remote old-timer's break deserted.

"Yup," said the old man, "but the Hawaiian name for it is '*Kalehuawehe*.' In ancient times only royalty were permitted to surf out there. ...The *ali'i* were the only ones allowed to own surfboards big enough to catch those waves."

As Makali'i digested this the waves they

had just ridden hit the breaks further inshore. They could hear the crowd devour each wave with a cacophony of barnyard screeches and grunts. The old man craned his neck to gaze shoreward and Makali'i saw the serenity vanish from his face, as if he were noticing for the first time the massing bulk of the high rises ringing the shoreline.

"You know," said the old man, turning his back on Town and continuing to paddle out. "I think it's an overlooked ability for a man to be able cope with change. I never could. Once the big passenger planes came, well..."

His voice trailed off. For a moment there was only the splash of their hands dipping into the water and the slap of chop on their surfboards.

"I could never understand how Duke was able to adapt to all the changes. Everything he knew as a boy was paved over. Yet he was never bitter. Boy, you should have seen Waikiki in the `20s..."

They reached the line-up and sat up on their boards.

"So is it true, Uncle?" asked Makali'i. "All those stories the beach boys always tell, that Duke rode a wave all the way to the beach from out there at Castle's?"

The old man nodded.

"Oh yes, but farther out that that even. He caught one of those giant south swell 'bluebirds' all the way to the inside reef at Queen's."

He scooped a handful of water onto the deck of his board and watched thoughtfully as it scattered into beads that glittered in the moonlight like dancing pearls.

"Couldn't do it today, I'll bet. The native streams are gone, buried. The reef's all silted up with suntan lotion."

Another series of fluid shadows loomed before them. But the old man, now somber and pensive, let them pass. The mood was contagious and Makali'i remained silently at his side. He tried to recall something Pop had told him about the old hollow wooden boards of the old days – something about a *haole* friend of Duke's who once built them on the beach on sawhorses beneath the coco palms. Was this the man, this elderly *haole* who had once come halfway around the world to be at the side of the great Duke Kahanamoku?

In a flash of awareness Makali'i suddenly knew that the old man sitting next to him did not belong to the realm of daylight. Yet he was not afraid. Hawaii was a place of ghosts, Pop always told him, but homesick and lonesome ghosts, ancestors who couldn't bear to depart from such a beautiful land.

"Uncle, you were so lucky to have Duke as a friend," said Makali'i, a little breathless in his determination to master his uneasiness.

The old man stared intently into the blackness. He ran his hands over the tufts of white hair on his crown. A glittering line of phosphorescence danced along the blunt rails of his surfboard.

"Yes, Duke was my friend," he said softly and a little sadly. "But I never really knew it was so until he was gone."

He looked searchingly at Makali'i.

"You're Hawaiian, aren't you, son?"

Makali'i nodded. "Well, except my Pop is half Chinese."

"You see," went on the old man. "You never know where you stand as a *haole*. The night before Duke's funeral his brother Sam and I were sitting down at the beach getting drunk. Just sharing stories about Duke and talking about the old days. Well, halfway into the third bottle of whatever it was he'd grabbed, Sam started crying.

"'Bruddah Tom, it's just not right,' he sobbed. 'It's just not right.'"

"I asked him what was the matter, and he began cursing wildly, damning all the '*opihi* and *kolea* who had leeched off of Duke's *mana* all his life, and saying how all the Good Time Charlies never knew how hard a life Duke had

had, always struggling to keep up appearances, to play act at being royalty when in fact he was poor like the rest of the Hawaiians.

"Sam swore he couldn't bear seeing all the *'opihi* and speechmakers gorging themselves on Duke's *mana* at the funeral the next day.

"'He belongs to us guys, Bruddah Tom,' he cried, 'He belongs to us – not them.'"

"Then Sam abruptly stood and loped off down the beach. I assumed he had gone in search of more liquor but ten minutes later he returned, cradling a small, square cardboard box. There, in the box, sealed in a plastic bag, were Duke's ashes. Sam told me to sneak over to the board locker and round up a couple of surfboards and meet him down the beach away from the lights.

"So Sam Kahanamoku and I paddled out in the middle of the night with Duke's remains on the deck of Sam's board, held under his chin. It was January and it was raining and very cold. Sam was blubbering like crazy and he was paddling like a maniac – I could hardly keep up with him. Then I lost my bearings, but I knew we were very far offshore.

"We laid Duke to rest then, just Sam and me. Out there…" The old man pointed out into the black void. "Out where the *ali'i* surf, at *Kalehuawehe*.

"The next day thousands of people watched as Duke's wife poured a mixture of flour and *keawe* ash into the water at Canoe's."

Makali'i sat spellbound, listening with swelling emotion as the old man finished his tale.

"And you know, the thing is," continued the old man, "I had lived with these Hawaiians – shared their surf with them, their food with them, their women, sometimes even their hardships with them. But it wasn't until Sam and I were out there in the rain in the middle of the night, hugging each other and crying as we returned Duke to the sea – it wasn't until that moment that I knew I had been accepted, knew that Duke had been my friend."

Makali'i nodded in understanding.

"You know something, Uncle?" he said in wonderment, still until the spell of the elder's story. "Sometimes when I'm surfing out here by myself – I've felt somebody on the board with me. Like they're riding along with me. Have you ever felt that?"

The old man smiled his agreement but said nothing.

"But – how can it be?" asked Makali'i.

The old man rapped the deck of his wooden board.

"Atoms," he said. "After all, we are all made of atoms. When we die we change forms but we cannot escape from the kingdom of the atom. Both Einstein and Jesus tried to tell us this..."

"But are you … how …" stuttered Makali'i.

"Oh, I put down the burden of life long ago, son."

Then from the outermost reef came a muffled roar like the sound of the great dunes of Time collapsing. Makali'i could just make out the plunging crest, now spreading into a widening wedge of moonlit whitewater. Were those slashes across the face the tracks of surfboards? And was that distant bellowing the honking of cars – or the hooting of exultant surfriders?

"The swell's getting bigger," laughed the old man, teeth flashing in the moonbeams. "Royal sport is afoot!"

Makali'i felt a curious mixture of happiness and dread and homecoming shoot down his spine and tingle his extremities. He watched transfixed as a tall square-shouldered figure came shooting down the face of a massive wave and slice away from the others, his mane of snowy white hair swept back by the wind.

Makali'i turned to the old man.

"Is that...?

The old man shrugged.

Maybe..."

Then the friend of the great Duke

Kahanamoku lay on his board and jerked his thumb seaward.

"C'mon, son, Let's go. I'll show you the line-up."

Makali'i followed. All the remaining noise and glare of Town faded with that last distance. He paddled dreamily toward the place where the wave had seared a phosphorescent scar on the ink-black sea. Where a booming voice borne of great lungs, half remembered from his childhood, was welcoming them.

Sanctuary

The surf was flat on the day Charlie Kessel decided to end his life.

A hushed gathering of friends looking back on his last day might have whispered of the many things that could have stopped him from doing it. Yet no one cared to look back. After forty-nine years of life Charlie had no friends, even among the little gang of surfers he'd seen every day for decades.

Perhaps if there had been surf that day he might have been saved by the old ritual of loading his surfboard and dog into the truck and, for the ten-thousandth time, go lurching down the narrow coast road to Talega Canyon. Then Charlie might have found some small waves to ride, or better, someone to fight.

Perhaps if the sun had been shining he might have stumbled along for a little longer. But that on that last day dawn brought only a drizzly grey mist. Charlie hated fog. Of course he could have shoved the .45 back into the drawer and escaped up into the sunny foothills. He often fled from the fog, climbing up out of the gloom to bask in the warm folds of chaparral scorched grey by the blazing sun. Squinting in the sudden brightness, he would look down upon the fog creaming in from the sea and survey his domain, the stretch of private coastline known as the Billingsworth Preserve, of which he was lord and master.

Charlie Kessel sometimes wished he had built his home up there in the hot bright hills away from the coastal fogs that bullied his foul temper. But the beach house was only a few miles from the reef at Talega Canyon – from his kitchen he could watch for trespassers. He had to live close enough so he could race down to the reef each morning before the sonuvabitch boaters and hike-ins got there. They never quit, those Outsiders. If you allowed them so much as a single wave they would come back – back with their friends and they with their friends, smuggling cameras so they could show the pictures to more Outsiders and gloat over the perfect waves they had poached.

The Billingsworth Preserve: its fifteen miles of jealously hoarded shoreline was all that remained of the California of his boyhood. It had once belonged to the Chumash but the Spanish stole it from them and when the Dons bled to the bone in a terrible drought the American ranchers snatched it from them. Statehood came and California grew. Developers hovered like vultures, waiting for drought or bankruptcy or death. It was not a long wait. The Billingsworth Preserve was again taken and subdivided and fenced against trespassers. Acorns and abalone, cattle and land – all had been bitterly fought over. Now pearl-handled surfers squabbled over waves.

It didn't matter now. Charlie didn't care anymore. It had been nearly three weeks since Wendy had left him. He no longer cared about surfing or Talega Canyon or the trespassing Outsiders that tried to steal his waves.

Charlie sat at the kitchen table, staring unblinking as the fog sailed in and dripped from the eaves of his beachfront house. The postcard lay on the table in front of him. A grinning dolphin levitating over impossibly blue water, *Greetings from Sunny California!* emblazoned beneath in day–glow script. The forced cheerfulness of it revolted Charlie. Any surfer could plainly see that the dolphin was in a tank somewhere, doomed to a life of hand–fed boredom.

He hadn't slept in days. His head felt thick, his eyes poached. His tongue tasted like a mouthful of pennies, partly from fear and partly from the pills he took for his back pain. The booze had run out weeks ago. Wendy did all the shopping – Charlie never left the Preserve. After his dope ran out he had doubled, then tripled, the pain pills. They were gone now and he was left alone to face Wendy's postcard and the approaching frontier of sobriety.

He flipped the postcard over again.

Charlie,

My attorney will contact you this week.

Please don't try to reach me

Wendy

What stung him the most was all the blank space. The few lines she had written consumed scarcely a third of the card. Squirming in misery, Charlie thought of the words he wished might fill the remainder. How could she have nothing more to say to him after twenty-three years together but a few cold loveless words scrawled onto a tacky postcard?

He flicked the card away like a horrid insect. It came to rest face up, the idiot grin of the dolphin mocking him.

The bright plastic colors of the card reminded him of 'down south' – of every neon-clad volleyball queer, of the garish bunting strung at the strip malls, of every arm-flapping valley surf cowboy – but most of all of his exile from the honking, smelly gridlock. Rage blazed through him, torched by the shame and frustration never very far beneath it. He had fled, hadn't remained behind to defend his home – he had been overwhelmed. There were just too many of them.

He lit a cigarette – he could smoke again now that Wendy was gone – and leaned back in the chair, remembering.

'Down south' was a painful subject for Charlie Kessel. Although born and raised along its shores, he had watched with bitterness its cancerous growth, horrified by the spreading concrete and poisonous tailpipes and greedy new faces. His father died in the mid–'70s; the family was grappling over his money belt even before his ashes had cooled in the little brass urn. Charlie took his pile and fled north to the Billingsworth Preserve, the last scrap of undeveloped coastline in southern California. There he found already established a small society of nervous uprooted surfers. They closed ranks around him instantly. So vicious were his denunciations of the invaders of his boyhood home that they all immediately forgot he was a newcomer.

A man's fear has no path but to hatred. Charlie spent all of his 25 years in the last redoubt erecting breastworks and looking over his shoulder for the invasion he was certain would displace him again.

"It's only a quarter tank of gas away, guys," he warned the other refugees, one finger held overhead as if he was testing the wind. "Hordes of valley goons and shoulder hoppers all backed up by frickin' lifeguards with guns. This is the last place, man. Soon as you go north of the Point it's just freezin' water and crappy wind swell all the way to the frickin' North Pole. We gotta make a stand."

Charlie was one of the privileged few who lived in the Billingsworth Preserve. Over the years he became the leader of a little squad of surfers that skulked through its gates to surf the perfect waves of Talega Canyon. Unable to afford one of the few million-dollar homes on the Preserve, they won entry by purchasing shares in otherwise worthless parcels of land: tiny, undeveloped patches of brushwood and poison oak tucked deep in the hinterlands of the original Billingsworth Ranch. Few 'Owners' ever took the trouble to visit their land – camping on undeveloped parcels was against Preserve rules – and left their grids of scrub to the wild pigs and rattlesnakes and hawks. The cost of a share was widely regarded as a membership fee. It was stated in the many by-laws of the Preserve that up to a dozen individuals could share a parcel. Each became eligible for the prized windshield decal that declared one an 'Owner' – and thus privileged to be waved through the gates. With one's name on a deed it was possible, for about the cost of a Tokyo golf club membership, to buy the right to drive into and park within California's past, where gathered each day a closed society more exclusive than any country club.

Each day the Owners came to the gates of the Preserve, lining up in their carefully worn Ford pick-up trucks. Charlie especially loathed the New Owners, yuppies up from Orange County in their shiny new Suburbans and tasseled loafers. So the Old Owners, led by Charlie's example, camouflaged their bourgeois plumage beneath the shabby cowl of battered F-150s, each stage-dressed to resemble a truck that a working ranch hand might drive. Rifles nestled in gun racks and grizzled little cattle dogs perched atop hay bales, spring-wound in readiness for cattle they would never herd.

Once waved through the gates they all filed down the pitted asphalt road to the driftwood shack at the foot of Talega Canyon. There Charlie held court, smoking a joint in the cab of his truck, glaring defiantly seaward, eyes slitted in patient reptilian menace. One of those sonuvabitch Boaters might try to drop a hook and sneak a few waves. The sight of his notorious Ford on the beach usually scared them off. On low tide mornings he arrived at dawn to keep away the Hike–Ins, maliciously whacking golf balls down the beach where they often clambered over the rocks to gain the shore at Talega Canyon.

Charlie had no job, no social life, no interests save that of the Reef. So he was always there first.

"Possession is nine–tenths of the law, man," he told the others when he was stoned enough to accept their company. Over the years this became their mantra.

He was the enforcer of the Preserve, the upholder of all trespassing laws, written and unwritten. It was, however, no longer an open reign of terror. The days of frontier justice had faded away.

"Christ, you can't swing a dead dog in this state without hitting a lawyer nowadays," Charlie grumbled, jumbling his metaphors in a haze of pot and unfiltered sun. He remembered with fondness the '70s, the unchallenged beatings and snapped boards and burnt cars. Charlie and his gang now waged war on the Outsiders in furtive campaigns of bushwhacking, of slashed tires and trumped-up arrests, of severed anchor lines and poisonous little notes plastered with excrement onto windshields. And the fierce and ancient crusade against the Dibblee Wharf continued, its hated boat hoist repeatedly sabotaged and unattended trailers wrecked.

But those measures no longer held back the flood. Anyway, Wendy was gone.

Charlie hardly put up a fight on the day Wendy left him. The first south swell of spring was sweeping into the outstretched arms of the northern points of the Preserve. Small boats already buzzed up the coast towards Talega Canyon and Shoalwater Cove, each bristling with surfboards lashed across their bows.

Wendy broke it to him in the kitchen while Charlie glared at the armada fanning out through the thick beds of kelp. He knew it had been coming. This wasn't the typical sandbox bickering of the childless couple. She was fed up. Their marriage was over. She was leaving him.

Though his 23 years with Wendy were blowing up in his face, Charlie couldn't keep his eyes from the boats. He counted them in growing irritation. In preparation for the predicted swell the boat hoist had been disabled in a midnight offensive. He had seen to that. All these boats, he seethed, must have been small enough to beach-launch. He scarcely heard his wife, so agonized was he at the thought of the unprotected waves at Talega.

"...It's not just the booze and pot anymore, Charlie ... damn you, are you listening to me?"

Wendy's eyes bored into him with such unflinching intensity that, startled, he forgot the unguarded reef. He turned away from the window and faced her.

"Oh, come on, honey, not the weed again!" he sulked, "You know I need it for my back. You know how much trouble it's been giving me. ...I'm lucky I can still paddle."

"You aren't listening. It's not the weed...." Now the tinge of pleading was gone and bitterness flooded into her voice. "Weed I can handle. Stoned I can handle. ...but the <u>hate</u>! I'm sick of it, Charlie! You're like a scorpion that goes mad in the sun and stings itself. You've poisoned yourself with your own hate"

Charlie said nothing, turning to stare out the bay windows of the kitchen they had shared for so many years. The fresh blue morning sky draped into the sea, bottle-green and furrowed with long-period groundswells that came oiling through the offshore kelp beds. His mind reeling, he saw them slipping backwards - Yes, it was strange, the swells appeared to be marching away from shore, away from him.

Wendy was blathering on, something about passion – about how he had once loved surfing, about how things had been different when they met all those years ago. Charlie barely listened, transfixed on the swells gliding out to sea. Yes, they had once brought him great joy. He remembered how it had been. ...Then there was the drone of another goddammed outboard motor flogging him back into the present.

He looked dully at Wendy, still rebuking him. The tone and cadence of her words seemed to stumble along as if trotting over cobblestones. It was a speech she had rehearsed many times but had been afraid to use.

"...How long has it been since you've surfed anywhere but Talega? You've painted yourself into a corner! I just won't waste the rest of my life with a man who's let the thing he loved more than anything turn him into a bitter old grump."

"What the hell are you saying? Is this about the money again?"

The State was under federal pressure to open the Preserve to the public, to create a park with campgrounds and boat ramps and numbered picnic sites. Charlie, who grew up cosseted by a seemingly inexhaustible trust fund, had squandering much of the last half of his inheritance on lawyers and bribes slipped to county judges. The first half had been spent, decades before, fighting the Coastal Commission so he could build his beachfront house on a patch of endangered surf thistle.

"I don't care about the money! You're not listening to me, Charlie. You never do."

His temper flared. "What the hell do you want from me?" The vein on his forehead rose, throbbing angrily as it did when he screamed at an unknown face in the line-up.

"Nothing, that's just it," Wendy said. "I'm leaving, Charlie. I can't deal with it anymore. The guest cottage is vacant at my father's – I'm going back down to Topanga. I'll stay there for a while until I decide where I want to go."

Charlie grabbed her by the shoulders, shocked. "You aren't going Down South?" he said, gargling with shock. "Come on, honey, you don't know what you're saying. I love you – you know I still love to surf. ...But you've seen the changes around here."

Wendy broke away from him and slid to the other side of the kitchen, keeping the back door near. She had packed some of her things into the trunk of the car the day before while he was surfing. She felt for the car keys in her pocket and ran her thumb over the serrations of the ignition key. It was amazing: All she would have to do was put that one piece of metal into the slot and she would be free. Reassured, she felt an overwhelming desire to be free of the Preserve right then, away from Charlie and surfers and the smoldering lawsuits. She was sick of being mewed up behind its gates. Her father's guest cottage was tucked deep into a box canyon alongside an enormous wall of ancient granite. Puma, deer and rattlesnakes roamed free, as they did on Billingsworth land, yet without the Preserve's claustrophobic by-laws and petty infighting they seemed more a part of Nature, not mere stage–props for a bunch of wealthy hobby farmers.

The cottage! How she wished she were there right now. Through her reverie, she noticed that Charlie's voice was slipping into that whiny squeak she hated, like he was back on the beach, fuming about some Boater anchored at Talega.

"…Someone has to protect what's ours. The Preserve would be overrun if we didn't. You know it as well as I do!"

"Protect the Preserve?" she smirked, "Is that what you call what you and those idiots do down at the reef, 'protect'?"

"Goddam right! There were fifty boats up at Shoalwater last week! And Nelson caught three guys above the high–tide line, trying to hike in over the Rigby land. They gave him lip, too … had to call the sheriff again!"

His eyes bulged as he grew angrier, one wandering to the side, giving him the lopsided gaze of an enraged reptile. "Look, it's simple. There's just not enough waves to go around, and the guys that live here have to make sure they get their share."

"Oh, bullshit, Charlie," Wendy exclaimed. "There's plenty of waves down there for all of you, and you know it. Okay, fine, you have your little hierarchy at the reef. Every surfer on the coast knows it, and you and your boys get the first pick."

Charlie pounded on the table. "Hey, what's wrong with that! It's our spot, goddammit! Will we get our share when this place is opened up and made into a frickin' state park?"

Charlie shuffled toward Wendy, closing the gap. She edged closer to the door, wary of the temper she had seen vented on 'trespassers'. Too late to calm him down – she measured the distances as her hand felt for the doorknob. It was best to keep pressing on the offensive, to pretend she still cared enough to be angry with him.

"Who jammed up the boat hoist again?" she asked. "Lori told me at the market. You did it, didn't you? ...Or did you have some of your cretins do it? What did you use this time, Quikcrete? Or epoxy again?"

He turned away from her, looking again out the window. Now he was the sulking boy, unjustly accused by the school matron.

"Hey, I didn't have anything to do with that. I can't help what the other guys do after a few beers."

She brushed away his denial. " How many guys' day did you ruin this time, Charlie? A dozen? Twenty? How many surfers went home bummed out and pissed off?

"I don't care," he snarled, " as long as they *went home!*"

Wendy stared at his angry face. Mottled and purple with rage, it's ugliness struck her like a blow. She looked away, astonished that she could ever have looked with tenderness upon that face.

"I'm sick of you and that pathetic little reef," she said. "You know, Charlie, I've watched and I've watched and kept my mouth shut – you've sold your soul for the Preserve."

She turned the doorknob while the other hand dove trembling back into her pocket for the car keys, then she slid out the door without another word.

When a man is at the end of his tether he only wants for a friend to hand him a cold beer and cajole him into thinking the world a better place. Charlie found himself utterly alone. Wendy was gone. He had no friends. The friendships of his surfing boyhood had evaporated long ago and in his adult life he'd made none to replace them. The isolation of the Preserve served to atrophy any vestigial social graces he might have possessed. Besides, it was 'uncool' to bring guests into the Preserve. An

Owner was allowed to bring in one guest, but a tacit code held that a 'true' Owner brought nothing more than a dog to any of the surf breaks on the Preserve.

Charlie's cigarette burned out, unsmoked, between his fingers. A neat line of ash had fallen next to the pistol on his lap.

The fog creamed ashore, thickening into drizzle in the south wind. The eaves dripped onto the swollen timbers of the deck. The dark kitchen without Wendy fussing about to county music on the radio was a murky tomb. Charlie recoiled from the sudden realization that she would never again stand there at the sink, humming over the dishes or bunching wildflowers into her brightly painted clay pots.

Perhaps he should light a fire. He dimly looked at the half–burned logs stacked on the grate. The gas had run out and he was too listless to get up and scrounge for kindling. Charlie sat in the cold dark house and tried to squirm away from the evil thoughts, muddled and hazy from the weeks of decay, that flooded into his mind. Everywhere he looked, the leavings of his life with Wendy crouched in ambush. The photos on the wall – Wendy on her horse, windblown and saddle–sore but beaming. Charlie bottom-turning – a decade younger and forty pounds lighter – on a glittering green wall at Talega Canyon. The unwashed dishes tipped into the sink – their last meal together – sneered at him. Her forgotten toothbrush in the cup on the counter. In the fridge the steaks she had bought moldered in their neat little paper packages, a meal she would never cook.

"Wendy, come back!" he cried, but the dark empty house only yawned at him.

He stood up and shuffled over to wall, squinting up at the picture of him surfing at Talega.

"That's passion, goddammit," he croaked, "Nobody knows that wave like I do!"

He thought about the reef, that lovely tilt of sandstone to which he had devoted so much of his life. How gently it shelved into the channel! Charlie envisioned every detail of the reef as if he was recalling the moonlit curves of a sleeping lover. Oh! how he loved that favorite combination of swell, when he could scoot on the slight surge from behind the peak as he stood up and slung into a turn. He thought about the crisp pungent kelp beds and the gold-leaf flashes of Garibaldi flitting about his feet as he waited for the next wave. Surely he loved that reef more than anyone else. How could he leave it defenseless against the remorseless trampling of Outsiders?

The drizzle turned to light rain now. The smell of rotting seaweed seeped in with the southerly eddy, the damp cold sea wind that made summers on the Preserve colder than the winters. Charlie couldn't bear it a moment longer. He had to get away from the house. Maybe if he saw the reef again it would be okay. It might be sunny deep in the cove. Maybe he could stuff the gun back into the drawer if only he could breathe the perfume of the low tide and hear the chuckle of whitewater as it washed over the smooth little cobblestones along the shore.

He thrust the pistol into his jacket pocket and went outside and climbed into his truck. He reversed halfway down the driveway before skidding to a halt. The surfboard …He'd forgotten his surfboard. Charlie sat for a minute, thinking. He flung the truck door open and limped towards the garage. The board stood alone in its rack, his wetsuit draped over the nose. It was a crappy board, factory-molded in Asia, one of thousands exactly like it. He hated it. But nobody worth a damn would shape him a board anymore. Over the years he had made too many enemies on the Outside. Wendy's saddle was draped over a sawhorse and the smell of leather and saddle soap welled up in him a flood of misery so powerful his gut knotted up with cramps. Fleeing the garage, he forgot the board and climbed back into the truck. He reversed out of the driveway and tore up the road towards Talega Canyon.

The windshield wipers flailed as Charlie nosed the truck down the ramp onto the beach at Talega Canyon. The visibility was worse here, the shoreline veiled in sheets of drifting fog that sailed in from the sea like full-bellied grey spinnakers. He turned off the engine and poked his head out the window, listening for breaking surf.

Nothing.

The hot engine ticked in the quiet and drizzle smeared the windshield while he thought. A foghorn sounded, the lighthouse up at Point Elefantes moaning its lament. Charlie recalled that a southerly wind often scooped away a clear place on the northern side of that cape that so distinctly divides southern from northern California. He was suddenly desperate to see the ocean. But the tide was too high and it was too foggy to continue driving on the sand. He'd have to head back onto the main road.

He was reversing up the ramp when a truck emerged from the mist and crowded alongside. It was Granville. Charlie detested Stuart Granville and normally tried to avoid him. He was about to nod and speed away but saw that he was blocked.

Granville rolled down his window.

"Howdy, Charlie."

"Gran'," he muttered, eyes straight ahead.

If there was anything Charlie loathed more than an Outsider it was someone who had been on the Preserve longer than him. Stuart Granville was born in 1951 on a ranch further inland – a bona fide ranch – and was one of the first local boys to discover, back in the '60s, the surfing potential of the hidden coast. A diffident rural teen, he looked forward to the weekends, secretly wishing that other surfers might drive up from Santa Monica or Dana Point so he could sidle up to them and listen to their talk of

Malibu or Trestle's. On weekdays and during the long cold winter he had surfed alone.

"Hey, I'm sorry about … I heard about Wendy," he said. " Damned shame. Anything I can do?"

Charlie's haggard grey face turned to stare at him, and Granville saw a blankness in the sunken eyes that gave him a chill. The strain of the past three weeks had ruined him. All the features Charlie had cultivated to make him appear more intimidating – the Fu Manchu moustache, the barrel chest, the football of a head shaved shiny – rendered him now a merely pathetic, almost comic figure.

Charlie refused to look at Granville.

"No, I just need to be alone."

Charlie Kessel had always wanted to be alone, thought Granville. He always wondered why Charlie hadn't left years ago. He had the money: If he wanted solitude, why the hell didn't he pack it up and go to New Zealand or Rarotonga? It wasn't as if they all hadn't seen it coming. By the early '70s the secret was over. Outsiders were trickling into the Preserve. Handfuls became dozens, and dozens multiplied into hundreds. For a while Granville tried, like the others, to stave off the invasion. The Billingsworth Surf Club was formed, ostensibly to promote the image of surfers amongst the entrenched cattlemen, though its real purpose was to collect the loose jumble of surfers and bundle them into a solid thew of Regulators. They adopted plain black wetsuits as their Black Shirts, a uniform showing both solidarity and their renunciation of Down South.

At first, Outsiders ducked past the gates when the guard was eating lunch or chasing stray cattle. The Owners chained and locked the main gate. The chains were hacksawed in midnight sorties, and so a guard shack was built, manned by a mean, limping little cowhand with a shotgun and a hatred of 'longhairs'. The beach became the next salient in the battle. Hike-ins were arrested and fined when they strayed even a foot up from the wet sand and county judges were bought off to make it stick. The Hike-in culture soon fizzled – rumors of rough treatment, even beatings spread far up and down the coast. Next the trespassers took to boating in. The Owners watched with impotent fury the violation of their claim by fleets of rickety little Glaspars and ChrisCrafts. They went into a huddle. But a running campaign against the boat hoist brought mixed results, and sending a diver out to cut anchor lines brought scattershot results and was often dangerous. Urchin divers, surfing during the evening's anchorage, were a rough-and-ready lot who were wise to the ploy and armed with shotguns. They watched for the bubbles.

So, behind the breastworks the little band of Owners gathered at Talega Canyon each day there was surf. There was no camaraderie, no hooting at another's rides and, therefore, no real bonds of friendship. If Blackie with the tar-smudged white surfboard ran into Bill with the tar-smudged white surfboard at the old general store in Bolton, no words were spoken, no handshakes or small talk exchanged, merely a slight lifting of the head as the barest acknowledgment the other existed. Few would have been able to recognize any of the others unpeeled from their black rubber uniforms. Each looked down upon the other from whatever perch he occupied in the caste system that sorted out Resident Owners, Old Owners, New Owners and One-Twelfth Deeders. Only in their mutual hate of Boaters and Hiker-Ins were they united. Each suspected the other of secretly plotting to bring guests - grasping Outsiders - into the Preserve.

Each day they parked cheek-and-jowl on the same strip of sand, to bob packed together in the small line-up, greedily snatching in turn at the delicate curls according to a pecking order both unspoken and unyielding. Perhaps they once surfed as grinning hooting boys, perhaps they had once thrilled to the spices of youthful camaraderie, but now they rode the waves under the uneasy truce of warring desert tribes who, finding themselves at the sole oasis in a trackless desert, drink from the precious wells with one suspicious eye cocked at those whom they would normally butcher at the slightest insult.

After a few years the range war began to seem absurd to Granville. One day he looked in the mirror and faced a 50-year-old man with a creased walnut of a forehead and little tufts of hair growing out of his ears. It was not the face of a man who could slash a tire. He started making excuses to not go surfing, and dreaded the trumpeted big swells that brought crowds and conflict. He backed out of the fray and retreated to what remained of the family ranch, now an avocado orchard deep in the Preserve. He was a reasonable man. By the mid '80s it was clear that the ramparts were overrun, and the little band of Owners never would be able to seal the breaches.

He stopped surfing at Talega Canyon. It wasn't the best or longest wave on the Preserve – a short ride, simple to surf – but its small reef and compact takeoff zone made it easy for the Owners to control, easy to cut off and squeeze out trespassers.

Granville began spending more time on his land and took to surfing the lesser breaks in the Preserve. Away from the skirmishes and the draining necessity of daily retaining his place in the pecking order, his serenity returned. Charlie and the Talega gang ridiculed him behind his back, mocking him for an old man who had lost both his nerve and his spot in the line–up.

Granville cleared his throat and said, "Hey, I'm just taking the dogs out for a swim since it's flat. Want to walk up the beach a ways?"

"No."

He dug at the sand with his toe and thought for a minute.

"Maybe you should try and get out of here for a while, Charlie. Go on a trip. When was the last time you drove up to Mendo? You used to like it up there."

Charlie tried to look at Granville but it was too much trouble to turn his head and refocus his eyes.

"I can't."

He couldn't leave anymore; he was notorious. There were a lot of people Outside who would like to catch him away from his little army on the Preserve.

"Come on, go away for a while," urged Granville. "Go away and show her you can change. Wendy will come back. Write her a letter from somewhere – anywhere but here – and maybe..."

Charlie snapped his head to face him. "What the hell do you know about it!" he roared.

"I just thought it would help if you got away from here for awhile. This place... well, it hasn't been good for you."

Charlie clenched the steering wheel so tightly that his knucklebones shone white through his skin.

"I love this place ... more ... than ... anyone!"

Granville looked away, vexed at his own rising temper. He cursed the whim that had brought him to the beach at that instant. He exhaled deeply.

"Just because you love something," he said, "doesn't mean you can't ruin it."

Wendy flashed into Charlie's mind. The thought of her robbed him of the energy to remain angry. He leaned forward and rested his forehead on the steering wheel.

"Besides," he moaned, "there's nowhere else to go. You don't know what it was like to have to leave ... you grew up here, you don't know what it was like down south."

Granville stared at him for a moment. "You're wrong, Charlie," he said softly. "I do know – you brought it with you."

Enraged, Charlie screeched one brutal expletive and revved his truck back to life. He ground it into reverse and in a howl of scraping gear teeth backed around Granville's truck.

He was sobbing by the time the truck skidded to a halt beneath the lighthouse standing at the tip of Point Elefantes. He got out of the cab and tottered to the brink of the sea cliffs, the northern boundary of the Preserve and the first shore in California to blacken with the chill of northern gales. The wind blew on his back now as he faced north, the fog warping around him and curling over the lip of the cliff as if phantoms sucked into oblivion.

The sea was somewhere below – he heard it shudder and breathe as though a living thing. He peered over the edge. The foghorn bellowed and made him start. At first there was only a formless swirl of grey and black and white. Then he could make out the ancient wreck of the *Mariner*. Through gaps in the mist he spied its ruined hulk, pinned forever on the evil black claws of rock. Thick heads of bull kelp jigged in the chop, their slick brown manes whirling as each wave hurled against the hull.

Suddenly seasick from vertigo and pills and the motion below, Charlie sank to his knees and vomited into the mass of iceplant ringing the cliff edge. He knelt there, spitting and retching for a few minutes before he noticed nearby a faded sign atop a worm–eaten post, recognizing with a pang of nostalgia the old '70s print: "*No Trespassing! Billingsworth Preserve Association.*"

He crawled up to the sign, remembering Wendy's accusation – "*How many guys' day did you ruin this time, Charlie?*" He tore the sign from its rotting post and flung it over the cliff.

"There, Wendy, see?" he croaked, watching it sail into the blackness. "I'm opening the gates for every Hike-in kook and his dog!"

Charlie dropped down again, face pressed into the iceplant, and wept tears of self-pity. Here was the very last foot of his native southland – he had nowhere else to go, no one to go there with. Wendy was gone. He was more afraid than he'd ever been in his life.

Sometime later – perhaps a few minutes, perhaps an hour – he felt warmth on his neck and squinted up to see sunlight boring through a thinning fogbank. The wind was freshening now, beating back the smell of rotting kelp. A northwest wind blew in from the open sea, cleaving huge canyons of sky from the fog. The ocean began to appear, first black and pitted like hammered steel, then greener and greener as the sun played across the surface.

Charlie climbed unsteadily to his feet. Spellbound, he watched the sea-change as if he had never before seen the ocean. Soon the horizon was clear, the last of the fog torn into little puffs and blown south into the embayed waters behind the cape.

Charlie gaped at the unbounded span of ocean charging towards him, a nation of chiseled jade flecked with tumbling whitecaps. The wind tasted clean and cold and set his jacket flapping and his eyes watering. It was as if he was on the prow of a ship facing the limitless Pacific, its energy vibrating up through the rock to his feet. The ocean was a new thing to him at that moment. It seemed so immense, so magnificent. He had a sudden flash of how it had first appeared to him when he was a child.

The reef he had devoted his life to, a little leeward reef tucked deep behind the gates of the Preserve, suddenly melted into squalid insignificance.

Charlie Kessel wobbled in the freshening wind. It had cleared his head, though his knees were starting to throb with pain – always the prelude to another spell of crippling back pain.

In his jacket pocket the shape of the .45 pressed against his middle-aged potbelly, the cold metal making him acutely aware of how flabby he had become.

He'd have the devil of a backache soon if he didn't find some pot or get more back pills. He'd have to drive into town to fill the prescription. ...Probably the druggist would have heard about Wendy.

The foghorn lowed down at him with bovine indifference.

"Oh, what the hell..." he said, pulling the pistol from his jacket. It felt as heavy as a dead star and swung upward locked in its own primordial gravity and in one unchecked motion the muzzle found his temple.

The shot cracked over the fields and clattered up into the warm bright hills where he might have been happy.

Made in the USA
San Bernardino, CA
26 June 2013